I0784146

ESCAPING THE WAR:
BASED ON A TRUE STORY FROM WORLD WAR II
By Paul W. Alexi

ISBN: 979-8-218-61091-3

Edited by Rich Donnelly & Judy White
Cover design and layout by Bob Paltrow Design
Cover photographs by E.J. Wergin

While inspired by a true story, this is a work of fiction. All names, characters,
places, and incidents portrayed are fictitious within the context of historical events.
No identification with actual persons (living or deceased), places or locations
should be inferred. Any resemblance is purely coincidental.

ESCAPING THE WAR

BASED ON A TRUE STORY FROM WORLD WAR II

—— PAUL W. ALEXI ——

February 19, 1945

It was the quiet time of the morning. British planes, having completed their nightly bombing runs, were returning to their airbases in England, while the Americans had yet to arrive. Rudi welcomed the silence as he got out of bed and slowly stood up. It had been a rare night of drinking. Despite the food rationing and shortages of everything else, somehow there was always enough alcohol.

It's a damn mystery, he thought to himself as he went to the washroom to clear his head and get ready for the day.

It was necessary to be up early. As the chief weather officer, he was responsible for preparing forecasts for the small airfield outside of Hustedt. When fuel was available, the Luftwaffe still launched aircraft, even though the Allied armies were approaching the German border to the west and the Russians were nearing Berlin.

Stationed at the airfield were a training squadron and a night fighter group that functioned sporadically and both would need weather reports after breakfast. The airfield itself was nothing special, having been hastily built in the mid-1930s primarily to train pilots. The runway was grass and there were no hangars for the aircraft per se, just camouflaged sheds to provide protection from the elements. The aircraft were parked on the south side of the landing strip in the forest away from the barracks. A Flak 8.8cm anti-aircraft battery, with searchlights, was hidden nearby. Deeper in the forest was an ammunition dump.

Because Rudi was in charge of the airfield weather staff, he had a small room to himself in one of the primitive one-story barracks. The three dozen or so barracks were clustered together and arranged in semi-circles under pine trees on the east side of the runway and connected by gravel lanes. Running next to the barracks complex were a country road and railroad tracks that led south to Celle, the nearest town. With faded wood siding, flat roofs and coal stoves for heat, the simple barracks were comfortable although a bit cramped. Small logs had been cut to make a low fence in front of each building. Combined with additional housing in the surrounding villages, the airfield accommodated a few hundred personnel. The area was almost idyllic, with forest in all directions bordering a patchwork of farmers' fields.

Approaching his thirty-fifth birthday, Rudi was of average height with blue eyes and an early receding hairline. When he smiled, a gold tooth glinted from a pre-molar. He was fit, a consequence of having started work as a boy in his family's commercial fishery and on their small farm located on the island of Wolin in the delta of the Oder River. His family owned three large wooden skiffs, powered only by oar and a sprit rig sail. With these, Rudi and his father fished for eel and the many fish that plied the Oder River.

When not used for fishing, the boats were rowed to islands in the delta to collect hay for their cows. Most of the villagers owned plots of land on the islands for this purpose. During the hot summers, amongst clouds of mosquitoes, Rudi and his father would work together using scythes to cut the hay, which they then loaded onto a skiff and rowed back to the farm. Everything was done by hand, and the hard labor at a young age had made him strong. In the village school he'd been a top gymnast.

Rudi wasn't a showoff by nature, but sometimes for fun, at parties and after a few drinks, he could still press himself into a handstand from a chair. He'd done one last night. Members from his weather group and some of the aircraft mechanics had partied and played a number of drinking games, including a raucous round where two people raced each other: one trying to empty a glass of beer with a spoon, while another ate a dry bun. Usually the one eating the bun lost as their mouth dried out.

Finished dressing, Rudi left for the mess hall in the middle of the barracks cluster. Low on the horizon, the early morning sun shone pink through the tall pine trees as he stepped out into the crisp air. It had been one of the coldest winters in memory, and its effects still lingered. Sidestepping a patch of snow on the narrow walkway, he turned down the gravel lane and joined others walking to the mess hall for breakfast or start their shifts. He was wearing the uniform of a Luftwaffe officer, but this was an anomaly. He had joined the German weather service as a civilian well before the war started, interested in making a career of it. However, as soon as the war started the weather service had been absorbed into the Luftwaffe. One needs to know the weather in order to fight a war.

Being older and pragmatic, Rudi had never been particularly enamored with the military, finding some military conventions to be ridiculous and its authority overbearing. He'd always been comfortable defying traditional conventions when it was necessary or suited him—not an attitude favored by any military.

When the weather service came under the command of the Luftwaffe, he and other weather technicians were sent to an airfield outside of Hamburg to undertake military training. There they received additional instruction on a wide variety of subjects: astronomy, meteorology, how to collect and interpret weather data, including adapting their knowledge of the weather to the military environment. Because they could be assigned to serve as members of an aircrew, they also received flight orientation courses and weapons training, as some aircraft were armed. Importantly, there were navigation courses as the weather officer doubled as the aircraft's navigator. Rudi enjoyed the classes, and they reinforced his idea of making a career out of the weather service.

The only thing he detested was the early morning physical training, especially the instructor, who was a bully. Each morning the class of about fifty was made to run laps around the perimeter of the airfield. He was in good shape and capable of running it just fine, but in his mind it didn't have anything to do with what they needed to know. Plus the instructor was loud-mouthed and abusive toward them. So every morning Rudi made sure to be at the rear of the group. As they approached the far side of the airstrip on the first lap, which ran alongside the forest, he'd jump into the bushes and wait. Once the group was on its last lap, he'd jump out as they passed, resuming his place at the rear.

Before the weather service, he had tried joining the navy's E-Boats, but they'd rejected him because he had flat feet. This had outraged him. He had already served over a decade in the merchant marine; had achieved his chief mate certificate and was an experienced sailor. This wasn't the infantry; he'd be on a ship! His short temper had told the navy where to stick it.

The weather service was a good fit, though, compatible with many of the skills he'd learned at sea. His position as head of the weather staff would normally have been filled by a formally trained meteorologist, one who'd attended university. Rudi's training was as a weather technician. However, wartime demands and lack of meteorologists forced many like him to be promoted to positions for which they'd be considered ineligible during peacetime. He had a village school education and multiple stretches at maritime academies to attain his certification as chief mate. Between ships he had spent his time on land always learning. Experience had given him a knack for predicting weather, and he'd stood out among the technicians training at the base, hence his promotion. Rudi knew he was too old to attend university now, but hoped that his experience would compensate for the lack of a university degree when he returned to civilian life.

On his way to breakfast, Rudi passed the entrances to small underground bunkers used when Allied aircraft approached the airfield. Some of those planes would strafe the airfield trying to destroy the aircraft parked on the ground, but most passed overhead on the way to bigger targets; like the previous month, when hundreds of American bombers had flown over the field on the way to Berlin for a massive strike, their contrails filling the sky.

Whenever possible, the weather group sat together in the mess hall reviewing the assignments for the day. Someone would collect the atmospheric measurements; another would draw and transfer that data onto the weather charts. Rudi would then collate everything and come up with the weather forecast for the next few days, posting it on the blackboard in the flight operations center. Because pilots usually had further questions about the forecast, he was the best one to answer them.

Combat missions took precedence over all other flights, although occasionally an officer taking a routine flight would try to pull rank and jump the line. Rudi didn't have a problem putting a higher ranking officer in their place if the flight wasn't an authorized mission.

The operations center was nothing fancy; it was similar to the flat-roofed barracks, but much larger and divided into several offices with charts covering the walls. Someone would also check if any reports had come in from weather stations further afield. These came in from all over, including as far away as a clandestine station located in Greenland. The data collected locally was then transmitted to Berlin, who passed it on to forces still operating. The information from Greenland was valuable as it was used to predict weather conditions over Europe a few days later and supported mission planning. As the war progressed it had also played a role in predicting invasion weather over the English Channel. With the D-Day landings by the Allies the previous June, that part was no longer needed.

He knew that there was another station on Spitzbergen as well. Having himself been stationed high above the Arctic Circle in the far reaches of Norway, at an airfield carved out of the tundra. His squadron's mission included gathering weather data and air-dropping supplies to the stations on Greenland and Spitzbergen. In addition to being the weather reconnaissance officer for his aircraft on these missions, Rudi also served as the navigator.

When making the hazardous flights to Greenland, most airmen favored the reliable Junkers Ju-52, nicknamed the Tante Ju, or Iron Annie in English. It was a tri-motor transport aircraft with short takeoff and landing capabilities, primarily used to transport cargo and airborne troops. The plane would be loaded with as much fuel as possible to make the flight to Greenland, air drop the supplies and then head back, sometimes just barely making it. For some missions the Junkers Ju-88 was used, a twin engine aircraft that served in multiple roles throughout the war and also had a reputation for being reliable.

Rudi was aware that the Americans also had a weather station on Greenland and often wondered if they suffered the same losses from the Arctic weather—half of his own squadron had been lost. He'd been lucky; after two years his missions were up and he'd been transferred to Hustedt, although that was not the sole reason.

Walking briskly, his breath condensing in the chill air, he decided at the last minute to bypass the mess hall and headed for the operations building. Weather reports came in via Morse code and were then converted into reports by the civilian staff. Rudi enjoyed listening in to get the latest information, but mainly he wanted to keep up his Morse code skills. He had taken to it during his years in the merchant marine and could manage a high rate of words; sometimes he was even able to identify the other operator from the way they keyed the code.

Rudi was still surprised to find himself in the Luftwaffe. Going to sea had been his dream growing up. Knowing that his sisters would marry and leave to start their own families, as the only male he'd be left to inherit the fishing business and farm. Having already started working at home as a boy, he had a clear idea what the rest of his life would be like if he stayed.

It was while fishing in the delta of the Oder River and the Baltic Sea side of the island; he'd developed a love for the sea. Despite the hard work, he enjoyed being outside as well as going to school in their small village. He was ambitious to further himself, and so it was frustrating for him when his father frequently pulled him out of school to help with the farm or to fish.

He realized early on that being educated was a way out. During the summer, tourists traveled north from Berlin by train to vacation on the sandy beaches of the Baltic. He saw how their jobs provided them with weekends off—eight hour work days while wearing nice clothes, plus vacations; unlike the work on their farm and fishery—up early, work all day, and then mend fishing nets into the night.

To make extra income, the family rented out a couple of rooms and provided meals to these tourists. His mother and sisters took care of them, but occasionally one would ask Rudi for a ride in one of the skiffs to see the delta. This gave him a chance to quiz the visitors about their jobs, how they were educated and what life was like in a big city.

At fourteen years of age he'd even run away from home, serving for a few months as a cabin boy on one the last windjammers plying the Baltic Sea. A couple of years later, he'd taken advantage of the tourist traffic when during the summer he left the family in the middle of harvest season to earn money in Herringsdorf, a nearby resort town. With a horse and carriage he picked up tourists from the train station to take them to their hotels. The money he earned paid for the tuition at the nearby maritime academy.

His father was well aware of his desire to get out, having also left their village for a time. At nineteen he had joined the German navy and served in China during the Boxer Rebellion. When the First World War began, he'd fought on the Eastern Front before being demobilized with a leg wound. Satisfied with what he'd seen of the world, he was content with village life and the rigors of fishing and the farm, which had been in the family many generations.

* * * *

Out of the corner of his eye, Rudi saw Helmut approaching. Tall, bespectacled, and gangly, Helmut looked every bit the school teacher that he'd been before the war. While not part of the weather group—he was the head clerk in the airfield's headquarters—he often sat with them since he came from the same town as Paul, one of the other weather technicians, and they now kept each other informed about any news from home.

Holding the headset to one ear to listen to the dit dah of Morse code, Rudi turned his head slightly. Helmut stood next to him and whispered, "The commander received a courtesy message from an old colleague stationed at the main airfield in Wolfsburg. They trained together as young officers and keep in touch. Apparently, an SS detachment arrived at their facility and armed some of his able personnel to send to the front. No details other than the SS might turn up here, and not for anything good is my guess."

That the SS would show up at the small airfield was news. And it was unusual, thought Rudi. True, various aircraft squadrons were always passing through. These squadrons would be stationed for a few weeks and then, depending on the war's requirements, they would leave and relocate to wherever they were needed. Even now a number of aircraft were parked at the airfield; there was a Heinkel 110, some Ju-88s, in addition to a Me-109 that had been damaged during a raid and then hauled off the airstrip and parked next to the forest. Painted a mottled camouflage gray, the wreck was almost invisible from across the field. Everyone at the airfield, from pilots and aircraft mechanics to the civilian office staff, was Luftwaffe personnel. The Flak or anti-aircraft artillery came from the Wehrmacht, along with a complement of teenagers who served as ammunition carriers.

"We should talk later," said Helmut. "I'm picking mushrooms after my shift is done."

Rudi nodded that he understood, knowing what mushroom picking meant.

Helmut often went looking for them; foraging was a way to enhance the sometimes meager food supply at the base. The airfield was surrounded by farms and orchards providing food for part of the year. Even into winter, potatoes could be found in the ground that had escaped being harvested.

"Mushrooms," in this case, meant that Helmut was going to check on a radio he kept hidden in an abandoned shed in the forest. It was a crystal radio set; they'd been unable to find a radio that ran on batteries. While not powerful, at times it performed well enough to catch the BBC signal after sunset when conditions were optimal, as the sun interfered with radio signals during the day. Thus the signal was strongest at night, bouncing off the upper atmosphere, giving its reception a greater range. The RRG or German Reich's radio broadcasts were the easiest to receive, but they leaned heavily toward propaganda. Still, information could be gleaned from them by reading between the lines.

Helmut and Bernd, head of the aircraft mechanics, had built simple crystal radio sets when they were kids. Together they'd cobbled this one together by scavenging parts lying around the aircraft maintenance shop. They'd managed it one night while the crew was off watching a movie at the cinema. Wire was pulled out of a generator from a destroyed truck engine already being cannibalized for parts. Bernd had come across some galena in town. At the time, Bernd had explained to Rudi that galena was a crystalline mineral with natural semiconductor properties, which separated out the audio portion of the radio signal so that it was audible.

Despite the radio's low power, it had the advantage that it didn't require a battery; power came from the radio signals. There was plenty of extra wire for the antenna, and headphones came from a pile of stripped aircraft parts. They'd strung the antenna high up across some trees near the shack, making sure that it was impossible to see, as it was illegal to listen to broadcasts from the Allies.

There was plenty of static with this kind of set and often two stations overlapped, but with it Helmut could get a basic idea of where the Allies were advancing, as well as the Russians. This information would be important in helping them establish not only how the war might end, but where.

As 1944 had come to a close and with the war obviously nearing its end, Rudi and Helmut had devised a plan to take matters into their own hands. The writing had been on the wall for some time now; the Ardennes offensive had failed, and Aachen had become the first city in Germany to fall to the Allies, along with other setbacks. No matter how you looked at it the war was lost.

They planned to protect themselves from the fanatics who wanted to hold out and would force them to fight in some last-ditch effort—guaranteed to fail. Together with Bernd and Paul, they'd come up with a couple of scenarios they thought would be feasible. The details could only be worked out when the time was right. For now, all they could do was wait.

For Rudi, the news that the SS might arrive at the airfield was unwelcome. It meant they might have to move their plan forward. He wasn't one to panic though. During his years at sea, working his way up to chief mate, he'd been in bad storms and tight situations. He could keep his head. It did cross his mind that the SS may know what had happened in Copenhagen.

* * * *

When they had leave, pretty much everybody from Rudi's squadron in Norway's Arctic spent it in Copenhagen. It was relatively quiet there and not bombed like the cities in Germany. Rudi had met a woman there on his first leave, and they saw each other whenever he was back. In her latest letter to him she'd written that an SS soldier had been harassing her because she'd declined his attentions. When Rudi next came on leave, one that would be his last, the SS soldier along with another one had come by her apartment unannounced. Finding Rudi there had led to words being exchanged and they'd directly threatened him.

During his time in the merchant marine, Rudi had spent plenty of time in dangerous seaports and sketchy places. Dealing with shady characters and a ship's crew had given Rudi a good nose for whether a threat was a bluff or real. In his experience most threats were bluffs, but his senses told him to take the encounter with the SS men seriously.

As he prepared to leave early the next morning, Rudi un-holstered his Luger and chambered a round. Saying goodbye at the door of the apartment, he descended cautiously down the four stories to the front door, wondering where the best spot to ambush someone would be. He moved quietly, as they might be waiting in the foyer. More likely it'd be outside, he thought, when I'm opening the heavy front door.

Stepping out of the building and onto the sidewalk, he found both SS men waiting for him to make good their threat. In the quick shootout that followed he had emerged unscathed, but both SS soldiers were seriously wounded.

He was arrested by the Feldgendarmerie, the German military police, and taken to Copenhagen's new jail. Rudi had passed by it on the way into the city as he and the other air crew members were bussed into town to start their leaves. Everyone had made jokes about it, and now he was in it! He was tried in military court, but with the woman's testimony confirming that he'd been threatened, the court had returned a verdict of self-defense and he was released.

* * * *

The incident was also the reason why he was at this small airfield in the middle of nowhere. He'd already completed his designated flying missions at the time and was anticipating being stationed somewhere else, preferably a large airfield. He was ambitious and wanted the experience for his civilian career—whenever the damn war was over. Instead, Luftwaffe Command had decided to send him to a small, nondescript field. The court's decision was in his military file, but few other than Colonel Steiner the airfield commander knew about it. Unless someone was looking through his file, he was probably safe from the SS's retribution.

Leaving the operations center for the mess hall, he ran into Paul, who was on his way there as well. If the group had a bona fide meteorologist, it would be Paul. In his mid-twenties he'd actually studied meteorology at a university. His studies had been interrupted by the war. Hoping to complete his degree he'd applied for a waiver, but had been denied and drafted into the weather service.

"Good morning," greeted Paul. "Join you for breakfast?"

Rudi nodded, "Morning! It's good I ran into you."

The gravel crunched under their boots as they walked together through the cool air.

Rudi continued, "Listen, I heard from Helmut this morning that an SS group is traveling to airfields and arming Luftwaffe personnel to send to the front. Where exactly I don't know, most likely to the east is my guess."

Paul nodded, "Hmm, I think so too. I just heard a rumor that office personnel at an airfield near Hamburg were being sent to Berlin to fight the Russians. Most were clerks!"

The fronts were collapsing—yet there was still a fanatical push to arm every able-bodied man to fight, from teenagers to old men, even though it was clear that the war was lost. Rudi and the others knew it. They were older, had seen the world and had never embraced

Nazi ideology to begin with; they were just serving their country. None of them had wanted a war. They'd been living their lives, raising families and looking toward a future when it started. Now, nearing its end, all they wanted was to see their families and pick up their lives again. There was no honor in dying for nothing. The fanatics and holdouts were prolonging the fighting.

At the mess hall they picked out a meager breakfast of cheese, sausage and bread. There was even some tinned jam, ersatz coffee, and tea. The weather staff would be by soon to discuss the day's assignments.

Turning to Paul, Rudi told him, "Bernd has finally agreed to join us. That makes four of us; you, me and Helmut. Maybe five, I'm not sure yet."

Paul nodded, "Bernd would be good and we need a mechanic for the car."

They not only needed Bernd for the car, he actually knew where they could find one. Bernd had owned a car repair business before war and was a wizard as a mechanic. He'd managed to get into aircraft mechanics school when the war started to avoid ending up in the infantry. Most of his friends back home had been drafted into the infantry and had died fighting in Stalingrad or were in a Russian POW camp—a death sentence of its own. He managed the crew that maintained the Ju-52 aircraft that were still operational. Married with two sons, his eldest had served with the Afrika Korps until being taken prisoner and was now in a POW camp in America. The youngest was still at home, helping his mother.

It was time to start the day, and so Rudi and Paul headed back to the operations center. Everyone else would have to catch up with them there. Rudi took his place behind the counter. It had a large surface so that maps could be rolled out on it and examined by him as well as the pilots. He picked up the collated reports prepared that morning to transfer the data onto the blackboard. The list of items was long: barometric pressure, dew point, temperature, wind direction and speed, visibility, and precipitation.

Across the office sat Anna, one of the civilian clerks responsible for transcribing the Morse code that came in from the various weather stations. The other women were faster than she was in transcribing Morse code, but Anna made up for being slower by making sure there were no mistakes.

As he wrote on the blackboard, Anna walked over to him with the last reports in her hand. Rudi turned to her and smiled. "Good morning, how was your visit home?" he asked.

"Fine," she confided. "Getting there was damn hard though, and it's getting more difficult all the time."

Anna's parents had a small millinery business in Salzwedel, only 60 kilometers away. Her parents were older, and because it was relatively close she went home often to help them with the store and their old house, built in the 1700s. She felt bad that they were on their own. Her sister's husband had been killed in the early weeks of the war in Poland; with a young son, Anna's sister helped when she could.

Anna loved her hometown and its 700-year history. Located on a small river that flowed into the Elbe and on to the North Sea, the town, while landlocked, had been a member of the Hanseatic League, a confederation of merchants and city states along the Baltic Sea that existed from 1200 to around 1600, making the town prosperous.

"The train only went part of the way," she explained. "The Amis bombed the last part of the railroad track and damaged the station. I hitchhiked. At least it wasn't far."

"Ah, how did that go?" he asked.

"Fine, except there were only a few rides and they were crowded. A postal truck picked me up and I had to stand on the back bumper and hang on with three other people," Anna chuckled, making a fist with her hands. "Luckily it wasn't raining. I can't believe I managed that. Anyway, now it's back to work; I'll talk to you later."

Rudi gave a short wave of his hand and went back to writing the last of the data on the board, finishing the forecast for the next three days.

* * * *

Anna and Rudi got along well, a friendship bordering on a relationship. She'd transferred to Hustedt from the Vechta airfield, located not far away. He'd met her last year while riding his bicycle back from town and found her climbing a fence into a farmer's field to pick apples. He'd jokingly accused her of stealing them.

She'd responded, "Yes I am. Who are you, the apple police?" She was direct and not easily intimidated, and he'd liked that.

They often saw movies together at the airfield's small cinema, or went to the nearby city whenever there was a concert. At the last concert they'd attended she'd worn a new dress and Rudi had complimented her appearance and the dress.

"Thank you," she'd beamed. "The dress is actually made out of curtains from our house. One of the seamstresses at my parents store sewed it for me. Maybe one day when rationing is over I can buy new clothes again."

But that was last year. With the front closer, there was now some risk traveling by bus on the open roads. A wandering Allied fighter could strafe the bus like they did the trains. Now when they went, it was at night or by bicycle, using the lanes that wended through the forest.

Anna didn't know about Rudi's plan with the others, but like everyone else she was thinking about how and when the war would end, and she kept up with the rumors. As a civilian, she'd most likely just pack her few belongings, hitchhike home, and that would be the end of it for her.

* * * *

As it was February, there were going to be days with low cloud cover. This was good as it kept American fighters away for now. On the other hand, it affected their flight operations too, although these were getting rare due to the lack of fuel.

One pilot walked in, probably the only one who would be flying today, thought Rudi. It was a courier flight to another airfield to deliver documents and other unspecified material. Throughout the day pilots wandered in and out reviewing the weather reports. Even though they wouldn't be flying, it was just their habit to always check the weather.

Paul closed his desk and walked over to Rudi.

"Let's meet tonight in your room," he said. "Maybe Helmut will have some more news for us by then. We should get Bernd to come over from the mechanics' barracks; we need to know if he found a car for us."

Rudi agreed, adding, "We need the car situation sorted out before we can do anything. If the SS does show up we might need to act faster than planned."

While most from the airbase went into town to party, attend concerts, or pursue the activities that single soldiers do, Bernd, being married, sought out car repair garages. He visited one regularly, not only because he loved cars in general, but he was curious to know, given the shortage of parts, what modifications mechanics were devising to keep the vehicles running. Obviously, some parts could be transferred from one car to another; others would require re-tooling to be functional.

He was a familiar face at one garage and a friend of Holz, the owner. At the same time that he was learning about workarounds on a carburetor or reconfiguring a muffler, he had a more important mission; to find a car they could steal, including gas. Getting their hands on a car was central to their plan.

In front of the Holz garage were several cars in various states of repair. Sitting to one side of the shop were an Opel 2.0 liter, a DKW F7 and a Mercedes 136. These had their issues resolved and now sat waiting to be picked up. Few people could afford an automobile, and so these were probably owned by the city administration or affluent residents. He'd made a point of finding out where the keys were kept—hanging on hooks in the shop. They'd be easy to reach. He didn't think the Opel would work for them. The model came in two and four-door configurations, and this one was a two-door. With four of them in the car it was imperative that all four could quickly exit the vehicle when necessary. The DKW had potential, and so he'd file it away for now. Ideally, the Mercedes would be best. He'd enjoyed working on them in his garage. In the end though, any reliable car would work.

* * * *

Darkness was falling, and windows in the barracks were being covered with blackout curtains when Bernd decided to see if he could find Rudi. The pine-scented air was cold but pleasant as he walked the gravel lane past barracks, passing people on the way to dinner or heading for their night shift. In some ways he had mixed feelings about the plan; maybe because it wasn't totally clear yet, and there remained some details to sort out. As a mechanic, he was particular; he liked all the necessary pieces to fit together. We just need a few more pieces and I'll feel better, he thought.

Stealing a car had been Rudi's idea, telling the others, "There's no way to know where or when the Allies will enter Germany, but they will. It can all change, so we need to be mobile in order to adjust our plans."

Entering the barracks, he walked to the rear where Rudi's room was.

These barracks smell a lot better than ours, he thought. His housed young mechanics, their clothes scented with oil and hydraulic fluid, and who had a tendency to wash less. I'll have to do something about that. He gave a quick knock on the door of the room.

"Come in," came a voice from inside.

He found Rudi and Helmut sitting at a small table. He pulled up a chair and they talked briefly about the weather and the goings on at the airfield. While they talked, Rudi put a half-empty bottle of schnapps on the table and three shot glasses. He wiped the insides with a handkerchief. Good enough, he told himself, and poured each one a shot.

After a toast, Rudi turned to Bernd, "Listen, Helmut has some news. It might affect our plan, but we don't know yet."

Helmut repeated what he'd told Rudi earlier about the message that the SS might show up at the airfield and what he'd heard over the radio, while "mushroom hunting".

"I don't think we have to worry about the Russians making it here," he explained. "They're close to Berlin and will focus on taking it. What's left of the Wehrmacht there will fight hard, keeping them occupied. As far as the Americans, Patton's Third Army is near the Rhine, so it's only a matter of time."

"Alright," responded Rudi. "Let's see what the SS brings. I think that what they do will force our decision. Bernd, any luck finding a car?"

Bernd told them of all the garages he'd visited the past few months, the Horst garage was the best option with a couple vehicles ready to go. The garage would be easy to break into and get the car keys.

Bernd told them his main concern was gas. "We should take some time to siphon off gas from the other cars. There are gas cans in the shop," he assured them. "When the time comes I could bicycle into town, get the car and come back. Or, do we all go? Which is best?"

Rudi thought for a moment before answering, "I don't think we should split up. The situation might be chaotic as it is. Anything could happen while driving the car back and you'd be alone."

"Also," he continued, "it might take all of us to get the car. We don't know if we'll run into anyone and what their intentions might be. If we're together we should be able to handle most situations. We'll already have made progress heading south if it comes to that."

Murmuring their agreement, both Helmut and Bernd nodded.

"Well then," Rudi said, "I'll fill in Paul when I see him. He was planning to be here, but must have been held up."

* * * *

Paul wasn't there because he found himself in Celle. About to end his shift, he'd received his mail, and amongst the letters was one from his sister in Hamburg telling him that his nephew Fritz was in the city on his way to the front. Knowing how erratic the mail was, Paul double checked the dates and saw that Fritz was likely still there. In the infantry, Fritz had been slightly wounded in the Ardennes. Now healed, he was being sent back to his unit. Unable to visit him, Paul's sister was desperate to have some news about her son and how he was doing.

Knowing that Rudi wouldn't mind under the circumstances, he hurriedly left the operations center and gathered his bicycle. It would have been best to have written orders from Rudi, as head of the weather group, giving him permission to be in town, in case he ran into the Feldgendarmerie, the field military police, but he didn't want to wait. It would take less than an hour to get there, and he'd be back that night. He knew where the troop depot was and hoped that by asking around he'd find Fritz. At least he could tell his sister he'd made an effort.

Taking the lanes through the forest would be shorter and keep him off the country road with less chance of running into Feldgendarmerie who'd want to know what he was doing. The short days of February meant he'd be riding at night, but the moon was bright enough to cast some light.

The depot was on the edge of town, easily recognized by the collection of trucks parked here and there. At this stage of the war, anything that ran was put in service, along with a few Opel 3-ton trucks and even some Fords. All had either tree branches on their hoods and canopies or netting to provide some camouflage from the air. Not much moved these days by train, easy targets for Allied fighters. The Opel trucks were the workhorse of the Wehrmacht, transporting and hauling everything imaginable.

When he arrived, Paul decided not to enter the depot through the main gate. Questions might be asked about what he was doing there, and so he walked down one of the side streets. In the dark, he could see soldiers were milling about and some entering a dimly lit café and bar. He followed them inside where it was packed with soldiers. The smoke filled room was warm, raucous and standing room only. It would be easier to strike up a conversation here. At first glance the soldiers seemed young, but upon closer examination their faces had the worn look, as did their uniforms, of those who've been fighting a long time. Everyone was making the most of their chance to drink. Sidling up to the bar, he asked the soldier next to him if by chance he knew of a Fritz Langer in the grenadiers.

"Who are you?" the soldier asked, slurring his words and examining his Luftwaffe uniform.

"I'm his uncle and his mother asked me to look him up." Paul shouted over the din. "She hasn't seen him in over a year and is worried."

The soldier nodded as if he understood. "Yes, yes, we are all worried, that's for sure, my mother too," in a slurred voice. It was clear to Paul the soldier was too drunk to help him.

Behind him he heard someone say, "I know Langer." Turning around, he faced an older soldier with a shaved head, a sergeant. "He's in my squad and is sitting over there by the door. You walked right past him."

Paul thanked him and began to wend his way through the crowd. He made eye contact with Fritz, who looked up shocked to see his uncle there.

"How did you get here?" he gasped. "How did you know I was here?" he asked again.

"You know—the coincidences of war," Paul quipped with a wry smile. "Well, actually from your mother. I just found out today from a letter she wrote. She wants to know how you are."

Fritz briefly introduced him to two other soldiers sitting next to him and then jerked his head toward the door. It was hot inside and stepping out into the cool night air felt refreshing.

"I'm doing alright," sighed Fritz. "The shrapnel wounds were light and healed fast; too fast for my liking otherwise I wouldn't be here now. In the hospital I tried pulling on them to slow down the healing, figuring I'd buy some time. A lot of the guys at the hospital were trying to find anything to stay longer. Nobody wants to go back; we're tired of this damn war, but I guess we're resigned to it."

He had just turned twenty-one, but had seen two years of war already and it showed in his face. At one time it'd been young and enthusiastic, but that was long gone.

Fritz shrugged, "Either way, don't worry about me; I'm determined to find a way to survive. What about you?" he asked Paul.

"My situation is as good as can be expected," Paul answered. "Forecasting the weather isn't inherently dangerous, just the occasional fighter attack. The Americans come over every now and then and try to destroy our aircraft on the ground. Otherwise, Hustedt is a pretty safe place."

Fritz thought for a moment and asked, "Hustedt, that's where you are? I thought you were in Russia that's why I was surprised to see you."

"I was, but then I got sick and they transferred me here after I got out of the hospital eight months ago. They needed a weather technician, a veritable godsend for me. I don't think I could have survived another winter on the Eastern Front," admitted Paul.

Fritz then told him some disturbing news. The name Hustedt sounded familiar. On the way here his squad had taken cover under a canopy of trees to hide from Allied aircraft passing overhead. A small group of SS soldiers in a convoy of trucks was doing the same. One of the SS soldiers told them they were on their way to several airfields, among the names was a place called Hustedt. They were to round up personnel, arm them and then send them to be integrated into fighting units on one of the fronts or maybe just to guard the Siegfried line. To the east was also an option as the front there was in trouble. Once the aircraft had passed over they'd all continued onward. The SS were heading somewhere else first. Fritz didn't know much beyond that.

Paul felt a brief electric shock at the news; it coincided with Helmut's news that morning. He was glad he'd come; now they knew for sure. He hoped by the time they showed up at Hustedt it'd be too late and the war would be over. They talked some more, and he told Fritz he would let his mother know they'd met and that he looked well.

Paul encouraged Fritz to write his mother, "It'll ease her mind in these crazy times."

After wishing each other good luck and a brief hug, Paul mounted his bicycle and rode quickly toward the supply warehouse on the other side of town.

Every night, supplies were transported to the airfield by truck, and if he got there in time he could catch a ride. The truck only traveled when it was dark. Almost skidding into the courtyard of the warehouse he saw it was still there, with its engine idling. He knew the driver, Ernst, a portly older man who walked with a limp from his time in the trenches during the First World War. He always seemed to have a joke about something.

Walking up with his bicycle, he shouted above the engine's noise, "Hallo Ernst! Do you have room for me and the bicycle? I need to get back to the airfield!"

"Hello Paul, of course! Throw that thing in the back," Ernst yelled back. "You can ride up front in the cab with me; Franz isn't coming tonight. You got lucky as I leave in a few minutes. I just have to check the paperwork in the office."

With the bicycle in the back on top of sacks and boxes of supplies, Paul walked to the front of the truck and leaned on the fender and waited. He lit a cigarette, the heat of the engine warming his back.

His mind went back to his time on the Eastern Front. It had been a horror. While not collapsing then as it was now, the front had been fluid and constantly moving. The Wehrmacht, while out-manned and out-gunned, especially after the battles of Kursk and Stalingrad, held off the Russians and in some instances even recaptured lost ground. The Wehrmacht had fought more strategically; making good use of aerial photo-reconnaissance. Film from these flights was developed quickly and used to assess conditions at the front and determine where reinforcements were needed, or if the Russians were gathering for an assault. This flexibility gave the Wehrmacht the ability to react quickly and move units where they would do the most good.

Weather conditions played a huge role, with Paul and his group busy forecasting weather in support of these movements. To function he'd started taking Pervitin, methamphetamine, helping him stay awake for long periods of time. The drug was widely available to soldiers to keep them alert, reducing feelings of fatigue and hunger; thereby extending the fighting capabilities of the average soldier. He took it in pill form, but for the Luftwaffe it was also available in what resembled a chocolate bar.

Staying awake for hours on end day after day, he'd lost weight, eventually developing heart palpitations. Given a short leave to recuperate, he left to visit his family in Hamburg. When he arrived he was unable at first to find his parents. Their house had been damaged in the bombings and they had relocated elsewhere. On the side of the house there was a note written in chalk, letting him know they had gone to his sister's home outside the city. They are safer there, he thought. Exhausted from traveling and having been awake for long stretches at a time, he decided to look for them next day and found a hotel for the night.

* * * *

He'd told Rudi about his night at the hotel months ago, knowing that Rudi had used Pervitin on the long flights to Greenland to help the air crew stay alert. He also knew the effect the drug had on you; once you stopped taking the pills, all you wanted to do was sleep.

"You won't believe this, Rudi, but when I woke up next day half the hotel was gone on the other side!" Paul had told him, "There'd been an air raid, and a bomb had landed next to the hotel. I was so tired from working and taking the drug I slept through the raid. Crazy! I found the hotel clerk and asked him why didn't they wake me up?"

The clerk, still in shock, had stammered, "We knocked on your door to tell you to leave for the shelter in the basement, but never got an answer. We thought you'd already left."

Both he and Rudi had shaken their heads at the near miss, the unexplainable luck.

* * * *

In the dark Paul could hear Ernst's footsteps crunching on the snow as he walked toward the truck. "Ready?" he asked.

Paul finished his cigarette, threw it on the ground and climbed into the cab, warm from the idling engine. Ernst turned on the blackout headlight mounted on the left side of the truck's grill, and with a lurch of the gears steered the truck out of the depot and onto the street.

Ernst drove slowly and considered turning off the blackout light once they were on the edge of town. "Since we always drive at night bringing supplies to the airfield, I worry about night fighters. They might see the light," he told Paul.

Paul thought it was unlikely an Allied night fighter would descend so low in the dark to take out a single truck. They were flying high above, searching for our night fighters, who in turn were searching for British bombers, but he said nothing.

They made some small talk and Ernst brought up his most recent adage, "You know, it's all shit, but as they say, enjoy the war, things will be worse when it's over."

At this time of night there was little traffic on the country road; now and then a car passed by. Occasionally they saw someone on the roadside pushing their bicycle, or pulling a bollerwagen, one of the ubiquitous small wooden wagons that people used for hauling coal or wood, or their remaining household goods if they were evacuating their town.

It's all miserable, Paul thought to himself. Maybe it'll all be over soon and we can think about rebuilding everything that's been destroyed.

* * * *

It was late in the evening when they arrived at the airfield. After a quick thanks to Ernst, Paul headed straight for the mess hall. He was hungry. The stress had made him thirsty too. Luckily there was some bread and cheese available and Lottie, one the cook's helpers, gave him a piece of sausage.

"For the sausage I'll promise you some sunshine tomorrow," Paul joked.

Lottie chuckled, "Oh, what does a weatherman know? My knee does a better job and tomorrow it's going to be foggy," she joked in return.

"Well you know the old saying, if you want to know the weather, look out the door," Paul told her as he made his way to find Rudi.

In the darkness, he heard, more than saw, people as they walked quietly past him. There was the muffled sound of barracks doors opening and closing, the murmur of voices inside, all dampened by the dense stand of trees. In the distance, over the horizon, he could hear the rumbling of a bombing raid somewhere with flashes of light bouncing off the overcast clouds.

He walked to the rear of the barracks and gently tapped on Rudi's window. The blackout curtains moved briefly, and Rudi waved him in.

"You look tired," Rudi noted.

"I am," Paul sighed. "But I wanted to tell you as soon as possible what I learned in Celle. It's second hand, but reliable." Then he related Fritz's encounter with the SS.

Rudi was quiet for awhile. "So, they'll be here eventually, it seems. We'll have to be ready. Maybe Helmut will know more in the morning. By the way you took a chance, next time I'll write you a pass. We don't want any trouble with the Feldgendarmerie."

He pulled out the schnapps bottle and a glass. "Here, you missed this earlier. Then go get some sleep."

* * * *

MARCH 7

The next morning, as Paul walked to the mess hall, he saw that Lottie's prediction had come true; the airfield was encased in fog. No flights would be coming in or out and, thank God, no air raids from the Allies for the time being. In this situation usually the weather group lingered at breakfast as nobody was flying.

With very little fuel left, not many flights left anyway. Still someone always shows up wanting to know when the fog will lift, so better to be on time, Paul thought. Entering the mess hall, he saw that Rudi was already seated at their usual table.

"I'm hoping to see Helmut to pass on your information," Rudi said in a quiet voice, "and have him check the radio tonight. We need to know about any changes to the front. Then we can calculate the distance south and how long it might take."

Paul nodded. The mess hall was filling up rapidly so they reverted to small talk, not wanting to be overheard. Any suspicion of what they were planning would be dangerous and get them detained.

From the far side of the mess hall Rudi saw Helmut walk in and get in line for breakfast. Helmut looked left and right, trying to see if Rudi was there. Finally making eye contact, he gave a nod of his head in recognition.

He looks stressed, thought Rudi.

Helmut was usually the calmest of the group, always ready with a soothing philosophical quote from Goethe or the Greek Stoics, and offering a perspective on whatever situation was at hand.

Almost through the line, Helmut reached for a cup of ersatz coffee and placed it on his tray. He looked at the tray and thought that if it wasn't for this damn war he'd be having breakfast at home with his wife

Trudy, who he affectionately called Tutti, and their dachshund, Plato. He enjoyed being a schoolteacher, but had hoped to be a professor of classics at some university like Heidelberg, lecturing on Stoicism and Epicurean philosophy. Over the years though, the class system had become a barrier for him. He came from working-class roots and lacked the necessary contacts that could pave the way for him. His abilities had brought him far and had served to overcome some barriers, but he was getting older. Already in his forties, he felt time was against him. Tutti was his biggest supporter and source of encouragement. "Don't give up, my dear," she would say. Maybe he'd try for the university again once the war ended. He missed her and Plato. They never had children so they doted on Plato, often taking him for walks along the banks of the Neckar River in Heidelberg.

"I hope it's over soon," he muttered under his breath and walked over to join Paul and Rudi.

"Good morning," he greeted them.

"You look like it's not a good morning," said Paul.

"You're right," said Helmut. "There was news this morning. I am a bit stressed, but then I always do when things change or I don't sleep well."

Rudi and Paul glanced at each other, wondering what Helmut had heard.

Paul turned to Helmut, "We'd like to hear this news, when we're outside. We'll walk you to headquarters and discuss it."

They ate in silence. Rudi acknowledged someone from the weather staff walking by and agreed to meet with them at the operations center. All three got up and returned their trays at the kitchen, put on their hats and stepped outside. Watching out for anyone in earshot, they slowly walked toward the headquarters building.

Helmut tucked his hands inside his coat. "Why is it still so cold? Winter is done, damn it! It's almost spring!" he groused.

He continued, "Anyway, what's the use of complaining? So, listen, I woke up very early and my first thought, like a premonition, was that I must move the radio! Lately, I've been concerned that my footprints in what's left of the snow could cause someone to become curious and they'd follow them to the shack. Not that anyone goes there really or would find anything, but one can never be sure. Before packing it up I tried to get BBC, but the signal was weak and there was static."

"Were you able to hear anything?" Paul asked, wanting Helmut to get to the point.

"The British 2nd Army is near a town called Wesel, and it could mean that Montgomery and his men will cross over the Rhine there and take a shot at the Ruhr. I had to look on the map to find Wesel—it's near Essen and Dortmund."

"What else?" asked Rudi.

"I lost the BBC signal, instead got our Reich's station, the RRG," Helmut continued. "They had the usual fanfare of course, now that General Kesselring is in charge of defenses on the east side of the Rhine;

big propaganda about reinforcements being moved to Mainz to defend the glorious fatherland."

Rudi had listened carefully. "So, from that we can guess the Americans are somewhere on the west side of the Rhine across from Mainz. The fact that the Wehrmacht is reinforcing it means Kesselring thinks the Americans will try to cross there."

"That's way south of us," observed Paul. "If the British get through the Ruhr quickly they'll head due east, right to us. We won't have to go anywhere, we can just wait."

"That's the best solution," agreed Helmut. "But the British will want to encircle it first before moving on and that'll take time. The Ruhr is a big nut to crack. The Americans, once they have Mainz, will move faster beyond it. I bet they'll head south as well as east. If I remember right, that's Patton's army. He's aggressive."

"All possible, at least things are picking up," said Rudi. "Our immediate problem is the SS. It throws a wrench into our timing. It's not certain they will show up, but if they do and evacuate us before the British get here, then the idea of waiting is out of the window. I'd say it depends on when they get here that determines our direction, gentlemen."

By now they'd reached the entrance to headquarters. Helmut turned to Rudi. "I need to find a new place for the radio. Let me know if there's a good spot."

"I'll ask Bernd," assured Rudi, as Helmut entered the building.

Paul and Rudi turned and started walking to the operations center.

"It will be risky if we have to move south," explained Rudi. "But if we make it, our chances are good of running into the Americans. Maybe find one of our units who've arranged to surrender en mass and we can join them."

"I hope so. I'd prefer to surrender to an army that recognizes the Geneva Convention than the damn Russians," said Paul. "When I was on the Eastern Front sometimes I feared that more than getting killed."

They fell silent; each lost in their own thoughts and bundled up against the fog, which made them feel much colder.

* * * *

MARCH 12

The temperature had suddenly turned warm, melting the few remaining patches of snow—spring was finally here. The four had gone about their usual duties, biding their time, when the news came that the Americans had crossed the Rhine at the Ludendorff Bridge near the town of Remagen. Helmut hadn't needed the radio to learn the news; it had spread around the airfield on its own. Now they needed to listen more often as events might unfold rapidly.

Bernd and Helmut had found a place for the radio at the maintenance garage, hiding it in a room amongst piles of salvaged parts. Instead of stringing a wire for the antenna, they used the metal gutters on the garage and drove a rod through the floor into the dirt for the ground wire. The gutters provided decent reception. At night the mechanics were in their barracks, in the canteen drinking, or at the cinema whenever a movie was available, giving Helmut and Bernd time to set up the radio. While Helmut listened, Bernd kept watch in case one of the mechanics showed up.

Meanwhile, Helmut learned that the SS had been delayed. He had heard it from Ernst when, after one of his supply runs, he dropped off paperwork for the supplies at headquarters. One of their trucks had broken down and a garage was taking its time getting it fixed.

* * * *

Anna was a fan of movies and often talked Rudi into going with her to the cinema. Walking up to Rudi in the mess hall after lunch, she sat down, placing her bag on the chair next to her. Rudi could tell it was one of those made from old newspapers. Most of the women were making them to use as shopping bags and to carry things. Sheets of old newspaper were twisted very tightly into strands and then woven into a net pattern with a handle. The bags lasted for a while and compensated for the shortage of materials.

"The movie last week was good," she told him.

"What was it?" Rudi asked.

"Der Kaiser von Kalifornien," she replied. "It was about the gold rush in California. You would have liked it, especially since you've been to America."

Rudi nodded, "That's right, when I was in the merchant marine, but only for a few days in New York. My first time crossing the Atlantic, I was only twenty then. I'd liked to have seen California, or more of New York."

"Well, there's a good movie tonight, an old one, Die Drei von der Tankstelle? Even if you've seen it, let's see it again. I want to forget the war for awhile."

Rudi smiled, "Of course, let's go. I can meet you here for dinner and we'll go afterwards. I still have some things to finish now. Till later."

Anna watched Rudi as he walked away. She mused about how it all had come to this. The war had started just one week after her 20th birthday. It had been a shock in many ways. She had become engaged that summer to Alexander, a lieutenant in the Wehrmacht. They'd met at a dance in her hometown and were inseparable afterward. They made plans to marry and talked about moving to his hometown in German West Africa, where his parents ran a karakul sheep ranch. Africa had sounded so adventurous and wild to her. Alexander and his brother had been ordered to Germany to complete their compulsory military service, not realizing that a war was brewing. Their obligations were almost fulfilled when the war broke out. A few weeks into the Polish campaign, Alexander had been killed. He'd received a full military funeral, something still possible in the early days of the war. Members of his unit had visited her to express their condolences and they had given her a photograph of his grave.

We've given our youth to this war, she thought, gathering her bag as she left the mess hall. She thought of her father who had served in the trenches during World War I. He'd never been impressed with Hitler and saw no reason for another war.

"People are told fairy tales, and those who tell them start wars that others have to fight," he'd told her.

She looked forward to seeing her parents again in a few days. Maybe after the war she would take up her former sales position at the department store. Anna had taken the job before the war to help with the family's finances. After it began, she'd added working two nights a week at an ammunition factory. It qualified her for extra points on her ration card, but weighing out the explosive powders had been unpleasant and made her ill, and so she'd quit.

Walking toward the operations center, her thoughts turned to Rudi. He was all business when at work and a stickler for details and safety. He liked reminding the weather staff of the sailor's adage, "One hand for yourself and one hand for the ship." Adding that, "Others depend on you to do good work."

She liked him when he wasn't at work; he was funny, had many stories and liked a party, but Anna had no expectations of a future with Rudi. The uncertainty of wartime makes you live in the present, she thought.

She knew he was married and had a daughter, maybe seven or eight years old. Rudi doted on his daughter, but had told her his marriage was struggling even before the war had started. He'd sent his family to live with relatives in the east, near the Baltic, after bombing raids had picked up in the west. Now it was the opposite, as town after town was being evacuated with untold thousands of civilians fleeing westward in front of the Russian advance; everyone taking only what they could carry or pull in a wagon. Whether his family was among the mass of refugees fleeing or staying put, Rudi hadn't heard. The exodus was happening in the middle of one of the harshest winters in years. It wasn't hard to imagine what that meant for the young and old exposed to the elements as they fled westward.

Alexander had died in '39, and three years later Anna had applied to work for the weather service as a telegrapher and clerk, needing to make more money and wanting to learn new skills. The training center was in Hannover, not far from her hometown, and she could return home on weekends. She enjoyed the courses, especially the camaraderie among the other women at the center. In their free time they'd put on plays, spending most of their time together. She had struggled to learn Morse code and had to spend extra time practicing to achieve even basic proficiency.

While in Hannover, she had a close call. Whenever the air raid siren sounded, the residents in her apartment block left for the shelter in the basement. One evening, she had just gone to bed after coming off her shift when the air raid sirens started. Tired and having already spent several nights in the shelter that turned out to be false alarms, she debated whether to stay or to head for the shelter. She thought, maybe this time they target Hannover for once. Suddenly motivated, she dressed quickly and dashed down the broad stairwell, whose outer wall was made of glass blocks to let in outside light. Just as she reached the basement, the bombs began landing. After the all clear sounded, she found the steps covered in shards of glass—the concussion from a bomb had shattered the outer wall. She should have felt elated that she escaped being killed, but she only felt exhausted. Nothing can be done; war or not, life still goes on.

In Hannover, she had a brief relationship with Gunter, one of the course instructors. A nice man, he'd reminded her of Alexander. She became pregnant and experienced a miscarriage, which left the bed sheets bloody. To their misfortune, the administrators of the training center accused them of having performed an abortion. As punishment, Gunter was relieved of his position and transferred to the Eastern Front near Leningrad. When she finished the course, she was first sent to the airfield in Vechta. She had a picture of her and Gunter standing on the railway platform in Hannover on his way to the front. The smiles for the camera belied the sharp pain of separation. Anna had written him until no more answers came. He'd disappeared like so many on the Eastern Front. The false accusation and dark paradox of a miscarriage being punished in the midst of a war that was killing untold numbers of people was unfathomable and made her seethe with anger.

* * * *

March 26

Ever since the Allies had crossed the Rhine River at Remagen, Helmut and Bernd had gone to the maintenance shed each night to listen to news from the front. They followed the daily developments and learned that a sizable bridgehead had been established by the advancing Allies and that several other crossings of the Rhine had taken place to the north and south near Mainz. All four men could feel the situation beginning to close in. Either the British show up or the SS.

It would be the SS.

After listening to the radio that night, Bernd had remained to do some work in the maintenance shed and so Helmut walked back alone. Nearing the barracks complex, in the fading light he could see some vehicles parked in front of the headquarters building: two trucks and a Kübelwagen.

"Shit," he blurted out and immediately went to look for Rudi. Walking through the barracks to Rudi's room he could tell from the murmurs that news of the SS's arrival was making the rounds among the airfield personnel.

He was so rattled that he opened the door without bothering to knock. There he found Rudi sitting at the table reading a letter. Looking up, Rudi pulled out the bottle of schnapps.

"Helmut, sit down and have a glass. You look like you need a drink," he offered.

Still standing, Helmut took the glass and swallowed it in one gulp. "I'm shaking inside, Rudi. I'm just a schoolteacher and don't want anything to do with this damn war. Is it them?"

Rudi look at him sympathetically, "Yes, it's them. Remember, that's why we have a plan and if things go our way, we'll be fine."

"Yes, of course. I'll be alright," murmured Helmut. "Letter from home?" He watched as Rudi folded the letter and slid it into the envelope.

"The letter is a bit old, but my wife and daughter are on the island of Usedom near my home village. They decided it was best to stay there for the time being, near relatives who can help," he said softly.

Helmut understood; the worry about family members was always there. "I hope they are safe. I should go to headquarters now; the commander is probably looking for me and it's better for me to be busy."

Rudi held up his hand, "One last thing. The section heads are to meet at the cinema tomorrow for instructions and then pass on orders to their respective staff. As far as I know pretty much the whole airfield is to be evacuated. Where to? We'll find out tomorrow."

Other than the mess hall, the cinema was the only facility that could accommodate large groups of people. When the screen was rolled up, the stage was often used for plays or announcements.

Before Helmut left, he filled Rudi in on what he and Bernd had been able to hear over the radio. By tomorrow it would be clear whether waiting for the British was possible or if they'd have to make a dash south to find the Americans.

* * * *

March 27

In the morning a notice was posted in the mess hall. It listed the order and times for section heads to be at the cinema. Rudi noted that the weather section was listed for the end of the day. He gathered his breakfast and saw Bernd sitting alone. He nodded and held up his finger to indicate that he'd be there in a minute and then sat down with Paul and the other weather staff to briefly discuss the day's assignments. No flights were going out today. The only remaining night fighter at the airfield had landed that morning; a Ju-88 with a radar antenna array mounted in front, giving it an insect-like appearance. It had run low on fuel. The lack of fuel had now grounded all aircraft at the field.

Meanwhile, scores of Allied bombers passed overhead day and night; the sorties were intensifying as the Allies pushed their bridgeheads farther and farther into Germany.

As soon as Rudi and Paul sat down with Bernd, he leaned forward and in a low voice told them, "I saw the SS this morning leaving the mess hall; there are about a dozen. From the insignias on their sleeves, they look like they're from several different units."

The defeat in the Ardennes had decimated Wehrmacht and SS units; leaving them under strength. Remnants were reorganized often with a new name or absorbed into an existing unit.

"Let's meet tonight after I've been to the meeting," Rudi said. "It'll confirm what we can already guess and then plan accordingly."

Bernd and Paul nodded in agreement; there wasn't much else to say.

* * * *

Rudi arrived early at the cinema and took a seat. Soon after the remaining section heads began to trickle in. The majority had been scheduled earlier in the day and had already been notified about what was next. Rudi had made a point of finding that out after the first meeting. It was what they'd feared.

All able-bodied men were to be armed and given orders to proceed to Berlin and to help defend the city against Russian attack. Pilots and aircraft maintenance crews were exempt from being armed for the time being, but were to be relocated east as well. The airfield would be completely evacuated.

Stupid, stupid! Rudi thought to himself. He was aware that there were many more German units fighting the Russians on the Eastern Front than the Allies in the west. Among the tropes that Hitler had used to get himself elected and to start the war was to promote a fear of communism. The chaos and episodes of anarchy that had followed the end of the first war, combined with the weakness of the Weimar regime in the 1920s and the later depression, had created a rise in support for communism across Europe. Hitler had billed himself as the only one who could prevent the communists from taking over. Even now, at the eleventh hour of the war, some even thought that the Allies should join Germany in fighting the Russians, as communism was seen as the real enemy.

What irony, Rudi thought. We're partly responsible, since our generals during the first war had sent Lenin by train to Russia to start his Bolshevik revolution and overthrow the czar. That way we could defeat the Russian army in the east.

Walking up the aisle of the cinema to the stage was an SS captain followed by two SS soldiers who then stood to the side. Rudi noted that the captain was older. By the look of the Knight's Cross he's probably been at this awhile, even has a saber scar on this cheek, he thought to himself. Those two soldiers though look young, probably drafted into the SS. Didn't have much choice.

The captain stood for a moment before speaking, "Good afternoon, I'm Captain Baumgartner of the 9th Panzer group. I'm here to provide you with orders from OKV, the High Command of the Wehrmacht for the defense of the Fatherland. I will be taking no questions."

He pulled a sheet of paper out of his tunic and began reading the orders. They detailed that all able-bodied men, regardless of age, were to be integrated into regular fighting units or assigned to the Volkssturm, the national militia.

The captain continued, "There are other SS details like mine in the area, and once you are ready to depart we will rally with them. Trucks will then transport you in the direction of Berlin. Given the uncertainty at the front at the moment, you will be informed of your unit upon arrival. You will pack only what is necessary. Tomorrow beginning at 0900, at one-hour intervals, sections will report to the headquarters for specific written orders. A weapon with ammunition will be issued to you at that time. If you are unfamiliar with its use, my soldiers will provide you with the necessary instructions. I anticipate leaving here in three days, meanwhile, you will stand by for any further orders. Understood?"

After the assenting murmurs had subsided, he concluded with the usual optimistic call for victory and that "wonder weapons" were imminent that would turn the tide of the war. And then added that anyone found shirking their duty would be deemed a traitor and punished accordingly.

With "That is all," he left the stage and walked out.

Rudi sat for a while as the others filed out. He should get back to the office and inform his section. They would be waiting to hear from him, but he knew they must've already heard what was going to happen.

There were six in his section: Anna, plus two other women; they would go home for now. The other male in the group besides Rudi and Paul was Heinz. He was a twenty-year-old kid assigned to them by the Wehrmacht as an all-around assistant. He was enthusiastic and good at collecting local data, which meant being outside in all sorts of weather. They often used weather balloons to collect measurements from the upper atmosphere. At a certain altitude the balloon burst, allowing the instruments to come down by parachute, which needed to be retrieved. Heinz would be sent to find them, driving all over the area searching. At one time, the Wehrmacht had made a half-hearted attempt to get him back, but Rudi had insisted that Heinz was doing valuable work necessary for the defense of the Fatherland, surprising himself at his hyperbole. The group did need him, but Rudi was also trying to keep him from being sent to the front.

If he wants to, Heinz will make a good meteorologist one day, he thought. I can't let him die for nothing. He would have to think of something.

Returning to the office, he gathered his staff and told them what he'd heard; how the airfield would be evacuated and orders issued for individuals or groups. Turning to Anna and the two women he told them, "You three will go home; wait and see what happens. My orders, along with Paul and Heinz direct us to an airfield near Berlin."

They had listened in silence. He hadn't mentioned that, instead of weather forecasting, they'd be thrown into the fight, a veritable meat grinder.

"Alright, let's wrap things up here and get dinner. Things will take a few days, but you should think about packing your personal gear."

* * * *

That night all four met in Rudi's room. Having anticipated this situation for weeks, their mood was somber now that they would have to act.

Helmut looked tired as he told them, "I've been writing orders all day and my hand hurts and I'm still not done. The whole situation is exhausting, but I'll sort ours tomorrow now that we have a destination. Are we still heading for Bayreuth?"

"Yes," replied Rudi. "Actually any airfield south would work. Bayreuth is as good as any and still operating. I'm guessing the Americans will at least make it to the Czechoslovakian border and that airfield is on their path. We could run into them sooner; maybe even bump into one of our units that have arranged to surrender."

"Best we can hope for then," said Paul. "I think it's good we'll be issued weapons. When we planned this last year, we never considered getting our hands on some."

"That's right we never did," agreed Rudi. "Given that we'll be stuffed in a car, we should avoid getting rifles, if at all possible. When they hand them out, insist on a Schmeisser MP40. The Schmeisser has a folding stock, making it easier to handle in the car and to hide too. I hate to say it, but we might need them if we come across a checkpoint with Feldgendarmerie or SS fanatics. They could question our orders and see through what we're doing."

"Oh God," groaned Helmut, "I've only ever fired a pistol for target practice."

"Let's hope it won't come to that," Paul said in a calm voice. "Helmut, the MP40 is basically a machine pistol and uses 9mm ammunition like the Luger; you'll do fine."

Rudi cleared his throat, "There's one more thing, and I know this is sudden, but I want Heinz to come with us. As a private in the Wehrmacht, they'll just feed him to the wolves."

The others looked surprised, and there was a brief pause.

Bernd asked, "Have you told him? I know he looks up to you Rudi, like an older brother, but can we trust him?"

Rudi explained he'd been thinking about it for weeks and had occasionally engaged Heinz in 'what if' conversations regarding the war. He felt confident that Heinz could be trusted and would want to go. The kid was smart and saw the handwriting on the wall in the same way they did. He was ambitious too and surprisingly, having grown up under the Nazi regime was not completely taken by it. His father was a chemist and, as a scientist, had influenced Heinz to be a critical thinker, swayed more by facts than emotion. And he spoke good English.

"Fine with me," Bernd shrugged as Paul and Helmut nodded their heads.

"Also, he knows how to drive a car; I don't," added Rudi.

"What! You don't?" Bernd said in a shocked voice.

"Nope, never needed one," Rudi explained. "I was always at sea, and when in port I was studying at one of the maritime academies. Where would I keep it when I shipped out?"

Helmut and Paul also admitted they didn't know how to drive a car, but thought it wouldn't be too hard.

"Correct, it's not hard," Bernd said shaking his head. "But now is not the time to learn. Anyway, we have two drivers, and that will be enough."

"Alright then, Helmut will make sure our names are on the orders tomorrow," Rudi said. "I'll take care of the rest. Keep focused on three things: the orders, weapons if possible, and the car."

"And gas," added Bernd.

* * * *

MARCH 28

Evacuating an entire airfield with hundreds of personnel takes time. And it soon became clear that the SS captain's prediction of three days had been optimistic. The enormity of the task created its own bottlenecks and confusion.

The headquarters staff worked at keeping everything organized as much as possible. Helmut, as head clerk, did his best to keep his staff focused on the paperwork necessary to transfer equipment and personnel to the front or other units, but they were falling behind. In the afternoons he would bring the morning's completed batch of orders for Colonel Steiner's signature. The afternoon's batch he brought at the end of the day.

Helmut now had the last batch to be signed. Some were typed, but since using typewriters took too long and there weren't enough typewriters anyway, most were handwritten. He'd personally written this batch, which included the group's orders.

Rudi had been adamant that Helmut, not some other clerk, write out their orders in his own handwriting. That way, in case they needed to alter them while underway, any changes they made would be harder to notice.

Colonel Steiner was a professional soldier and had been in the Luftwaffe since its inception. As a young man in the 1920s he'd joined a glider club to learn how to fly. Germany was denied an air force under the Treaty of Versailles after World War I, and so the only way to learn fly was in sports or glider clubs. The clubs were also used to secretly train pilots for a future Luftwaffe. To further this effort, Germany, in the mid-1920s, made an arrangement to train pilots at a secret airfield in the Soviet Union. There Steiner had learned to fly motorized aircraft and he later served with the Condor Legion in Spain. In the first year of the war he had completed his designated flying missions. After serving as an instructor he was later assigned to administrative posts at various airfields.

The staff under Steiner saw him as a good administrator and officer. He lacked the stiff self-important military bearing of some officers, but could play the part if needed. He was generally easygoing, but could be tough when necessary. He still had the élan of a pilot and wore his slightly crushed officer's hat at an angle. After having served at multiple posts, he'd come to like living the past two years at Hustedt. The area was relatively quiet; he and his wife had a nice house in one of the outlying villages and were raising their two grandchildren—their son was a POW in America and the daughter-in-law had died in a bombing raid. Deep down he hoped to stay here. It wasn't beyond him to consider the end of the war and what would come next. He even entertained the idea of flying for a civilian airline, such as Lufthansa, after it was over. He also was aware that the orders he was signing would place people near the front if not at it.

Standing next to the colonel's desk, Helmut handed him the last batch of orders for the day. He felt calm, but could feel a trickle of sweat run down his spine. In the batch were the orders that directed the weather group to proceed to Bayr. Helmut had spaced them out among the other personnel orders and hoped that their similarity wouldn't be noticed. The full name should have been Bayr-Berlin: the airfields around the Berlin air district had hyphenated names to distinguish them from each other.

"Ah, the last ones, Helmut?" asked Steiner with relief.

"Yes sir, until tomorrow."

Having already signed multiple orders that day, Steiner automatically began signing. Almost done, he stopped suddenly, looking at Bernd's orders. It was similar to a few others he'd just signed, including Helmut's.

An eyebrow lifted as he realized that order for the weather group all had the same destination, including the missing air district designation. Silently he looked up at Helmut.

"When you get to your desk you should fill in the district designation, Helmut," he advised. "Otherwise it's not a viable order." He looked at Helmut a moment and waving his hand dismissed him.

"Yes sir, thank you for pointing that out; I'll take care of it," Helmut said in a hoarse voice.

Gathering up the batch of signed orders he left the commandant's office, closing the door behind him and went to his desk. He plopped down more than sat, realizing he was slightly shaky. Did Steiner think it was just a mistake or did he suspect something was awry? he wondered.

As soon as he calmed down, he laid their orders on his desk and carefully filled in the rest of the destination; Bayreuth-Blindlach. This was south and not to Berlin. It was done. Bunching up the group's orders, he folded them in half and tucked them into his tunic and left the office. Outside, he took a deep breath. The warm evening air promised spring was here.

* * * *

Rudi had been busy. First he had to find Bernd who had a duffel bag of old Luftwaffe uniforms that he'd collected over the past few months. Sometimes a spare set was left behind in the barracks or an airman died and his effects had to be gathered up. He went to the mechanic's barracks where he was told that Bernd was probably at the maintenance hangar getting some personal gear. As Rudi neared the hangar door he saw Paul, who was keeping watch, and realized they were listening to the radio in the tool room. "Anything?"

Paul told him the signal had been weak and hard to hear; best they could tell the Americans had captured Heidelberg and some of the surrounding area. Further north, General Model's army was done, as the Allies have encircled the Ruhr.

"Ah," was all Rudi could say.

Having stashed the radio, Bernd came to the doorway.

"I need your duffel bag with the Luftwaffe uniforms—for Heinz," Rudi said. "We can't take him dressed in a Wehrmacht uniform since we are all Luftwaffe. Better he looks like an airman."

"Got it," Bernd quipped. He turned around and went to his office. He returned with the bag and handed it to Rudi, "Has he agreed to go with us?"

"Yes, although he's a bit nervous, but he'll be fine. There should be a uniform that fits him; he can pack it and change into it once we're underway. Now I have to find Paul to see what weapons he was issued this morning. Also, pack up the radio so we can take it with us. We know enough for now. Let's meet after dinner in my room. We have to figure out how we'll get to the car."

* * * *

At dinner, Rudi sat with Anna. Inside the mess hall it seemed calm compared to the turmoil outside with hundreds of personnel moving here and there, gathering gear and packing, ready to leave in one direction or another.

They made small talk for awhile, and then Anna asked, "I know you Rudi, and I don't think you're going to follow orders. Am I right?"

"I'll do what's best," he confided.

Anna put her hands under her chin and whispered, "I've seen you together with Bernd and Helmut quite often. More than usual, so I assume you are all planning something."

Holding up a hand she said, "But I don't want to know. Whatever you do, I just hope you will be safe. Please be safe. As for me, I'll be going home. My parents need me. You know, we were looking at a map in the office this morning and trying to guess where the Russians will stop. Do you want to know what I guessed?"

"Where?" asked Rudi.

"They'll end up at my home town," she answered. They grew silent at the thought. Who knows how this all ends, and then what about afterwards?

Rudi listened as Anna talked about her family and how she wanted to improve the millinery. Her father had inherited the business from his father, even though he didn't want it. Anna described her father as multi-talented who could have done other things with his life, but was forced by tradition to run the business. He was a member of a cycling club and loved photography, developing his own pictures. Calm and quiet, he seemed happiest shooting rats under the house when the nearby creek flooded after heavy rains, forcing the rats to scurry under the houses in the neighborhood and climb into root cellars. She thought it was because it reminded him of when he was most free; being in the trenches in Belgium where he was away from his demanding father and the business. Strange how we see freedom, she had marveled.

She told him the story how during the war her father had found two clocks in the basement of a church in Belgium. The black marble cases were ornate, but the mechanisms inside were strewn about. He'd collected them and brought the clocks home, piecing them back together. Now their gentle chimes on the hour resonated in the house.

Rudi said, "I'd like to meet him, he sounds like an interesting person. By the way, if I don't see you before you go, I'd like to visit you when the war is over."

"It would be good to see you when all this is over. You'd get on well with Father," smiled Anna.

They left it at that. Stepping out of the mess hall, Anna looked at Rudi for a moment. "Take care of yourself," she said quietly, turned and walked to her barracks to pack.

* * * *

Rudi returned to his barracks and found Paul waiting for him with a duffel bag. Paul told him that Bernd and Helmut would be coming by soon and described how the weapons disbursement had gone.

"Not the usual way, that's for sure," chuckled Paul. "We didn't even have to sign for them; they just handed them out. There were mostly Kar-98s, carbines and a few MP40s. I was able to get us two of the MP40s. One SS soldier tried to stop me from taking the second one, but I said it's for an officer and he let it go. There were also Panzerfausts and hand grenades. I didn't think we'd need an anti-tank weapon, but I did take two hand grenades."

Paul grinned, "Who knows, they might come in handy!"

"Good job! Schmeissers are what we need," exclaimed Rudi. "That should get us through, plus I have my Luger and if we need more weapons, we'll have to take them from somebody."

Bernd and Helmut walked in as they talked.

"Still have that bottle of schnapps, Rudi?" asked Bernd.

"Absolutely," and pulled out the bottle and four glasses. As he poured, Paul handed out cigarettes to everyone. They toasted and downed the drinks. They smoked in silence as Rudi refilled their glasses.

Helmut spoke first. He reported that the orders were signed and that all of them had been 'assigned' to an airfield in the south, away from the Eastern Front. He reached into his tunic and pulled out their orders, handing each one theirs, except Heinz's orders which he gave to Rudi.

"Wonderful!" said Bernd. "So now we are ready?"

"When should we—" Paul started to say, but was interrupted by Helmut.

"Just so you know, I am concerned that Colonel Steiner might have caught on to what we're doing." He recounted how the Colonel had treated the missing air district designation as a simple clerical mistake that just needed to be corrected, but he had also noted how their orders were similar.

"He gave me a long look. I know the Colonel and how he thinks; I can't be sure if he suspects something," Helmut's voice trailed off.

Rudi looked thoughtful, "I know Steiner too, and if he suspected something and wanted to act, he'd have done so right then and there. So I think we are good for now, but we won't waste time. As Paul was about to ask, when do we leave? I say tomorrow night. We can't risk being pulled into one of the groups being sent to the front."

"So do we go together or should I go and get the car?" asked Bernd.

"Let's stay together," Rudi said.

Paul held up his hand, "I have an idea. Ernst is still running the supply truck to the airfield at night, right? He goes back before daylight. I say we go with him into town and get the car. I know him well and can get a ride with him; I'll give him some story about meeting my nephew again."

"The rest of us can hide in the back; it'll be empty," suggested Bernd.

"Be tricky to arrange, we might be seen," Helmut said. "What if we asked him to take all of us. Could we trust him?"

Knowing Ernst, Paul told them, "He was a member of Der Stahlhelm, the Steel Helmet. A bunch of veterans from the First World War, nationalists, I think, and somewhat political, but they kept some distance from Hitler and his party until they were disbanded. He's certainly not a fanatic. I think we can trust him. As a last resort we could offer him some money, but on second thought, that would be a giveaway."

Rudi rubbed his eyes and said, "Let's leave it this way. Paul, tomorrow night ask him for a ride, but take him to the canteen for a drink. I know he likes schnapps. That will give us time to get in the back with our gear. We'll just have to take the chance we won't be seen; it should be dark enough. It's important to have him stop somewhere before he gets to the truck depot. We don't want to be stuck in it."

Bernd thought for a moment, "Just say you need to relieve yourself or say you're feeling sick."

Paul said, "I think I can just ask him for a ride for all of us. He'll probably not even ask why, might even guess what we're doing."

"Not yet," Bernd said. "It makes me nervous. Let's go with Rudi's idea for now. If there's a problem I'm not opposed to getting a ride at gunpoint if necessary."

"Oh no, I hope not," Helmut blurted out, "He's an old man and everyone at the airfield likes him; he always has a joke. I'd hate it if we put him in that position."

Rudi and Paul shared glances. Both of them had spent time on the front lines and had been toughened by it. They knew that people would do whatever is necessary to stay alive, as would they. They understood that for Helmut the war had mostly been about paperwork, and when it was over he'd return to his literature.

Not wanting to upset Helmut, Rudi waved a hand and said, "Not to worry, Helmut, it won't come to that. But to be honest, once we are on the way we might not have a choice and have to fight. Should that be the case, remember, whoever they might be, they are strangers who mean us harm. It's you or them."

Helmut nodded and said quietly, "Of course, of course, that will be different."

"I have to get some sleep," yawned Rudi. "Tomorrow I'll check in with Heinz and see if he's completed an assignment I gave him."

* * * *

At the same time that the others were discussing how to get off the airfield, Heinz was behind the mess hall in the dark. The rear of the hall bordered the forest, its backside lined with garbage cans and bins filled with grease from cooking; a feast for rats and other nocturnal animals. When it was warm, the cooks kept the back door ajar to keep the kitchen from getting too hot. The door was Heinz's goal. Rudi had given him the task of stealing some bread and whatever food he could get his hands on. There was no way of knowing how long they'd be underway or if they could find food.

Dinner was long over. Only a few staff where still in the hall to finish cleaning the floors and wash pots and pans. Wearing just his socks so he made less noise, Heinz approached the door and checked left and right. The kitchen itself was empty. Everyone was in the front, talking and laughing with each other. He had made a point earlier at breakfast of helping carry a stack of trays to the kitchen to be washed and noted where the storeroom was. When he slipped through the door, he knew it was immediately to his left. Inside it was hard to see with just the few rays from the kitchen light illuminating the shelves. He could smell the bread and carefully felt around for the loaves. Picking up a few, he placed them in one of the pillow cases he'd brought. It was impossible to read what was on the tins, but he knew from their size what they most likely contained.

He grabbed what he could when he heard footsteps coming toward the kitchen. It was Lottie. He briefly saw her pass by the open door of the storeroom carrying a pan of kitchen offal. She stepped out the back door and he heard the garbage can clang as she dumped it in and closed the lid. She came in and placed the empty pan in one of the large sinks. She started toward the storeroom just as someone called her name.

"Lottie dear, join us for a card game; we have cigarettes too!" a voice called.

Lottie paused. "Fine, how about a little money on the cards?" she yelled back. "Make it interesting." The response must have been yes as Lottie turned and left for the front part of the mess hall.

By now Heinz was sweating and his mouth had gone dry. He decided he'd done what he could. With Lottie gone, he grabbed one more tin and quietly went to the back door. Briefly glancing sideways toward the seating area of the hall, he could see them sitting around one of the long tables, engrossed as the cards were dealt.

It was cool outside and he felt relief as the sweat evaporated. Walking gingerly a few feet into the woods, he found his boots and put them on and then stuffed the pillow cases of food into a duffel bag. Walking cautiously alongside the building, he looked left and right before stepping out onto the lane, heading in the direction of his barracks.

In the dusk, people moved about, carrying one thing or another as the evacuation proceeded, and so his duffel bag was not out of place. He worried about the smell of the bread, but decided that if he hid it in the rafters next to the barracks latrine the smell wouldn't be noticed. He had hidden the airman's uniform there as well. If it was found, nobody could trace it to him.

Heinz recalled Rudi's offer to join them. Yes, had been his response, after only a brief hesitation. The offer had surprised him, but he also trusted Rudi and saw him as an older brother. When the war had begun, his brother had joined the U-Boats. A year later he had disappeared somewhere in the Atlantic.

He recalled how Rudi had sometimes joined him on his searches for their downed weather balloons. While driving here and there, Rudi had regaled him with stories of going to sea, and exotic ports around the world. He'd seen much of the Mediterranean and its backwaters, including ports in Africa and China.

Rudi explained that sailors were the most mobile people in the world and that the merchant marine attracted all kinds of characters. It took days to load and unload a ship's cargo, with much of the work done manually, leaving time for shore leave and various activities, such as smuggling. To make extra money, some sailors smuggled items to take advantage of the price differences between countries and seaports to make a profit.

Heinz's favorite stories were how Rudi had also occasionally engaged in smuggling. One time he had purchased a batch of cigarette lighters in Spain to sell when they landed in Genoa, Italy. One of his shipmates, Siegfried, or Siggi as his shipmates nicknamed him, was a prolific smuggler. Siggi had shared his contact in Genoa with Rudi and told him, "He'll buy all the lighters you bring him and at a good price. The Italians love them."

Walking up the street to meet the buyer, Rudi's small case had broken open and the lighters spilled out onto the sidewalk. Siggi had been right, the lighters were desirable and a crowd quickly gathered around him. Making the most of the opportunity, he began selling them then and there. Across the street two policemen sauntered by, oblivious to what was happening. The story gave them both a good laugh.

Rudi also described the Arctic, talking wistfully about its raw beauty, empty of cities and people. "The earth unchanged," he'd once said.

Heinz gradually becoming aware that at times Rudi was trying to determine his opinion on the war. At one point he'd told Rudi, "All I know is that I don't want to die for nothing—now that the war is almost over."

"Of course, nobody does. You're young and have your whole life ahead of you. Hopefully it won't come to that," Rudi had said.

Heinz told him, "My father wants me to follow in his footsteps and become a chemist too. It's all right, but I don't want to spend my life in a lab. Weather forecasting is interesting, but maybe not for me."

"What then?" Rudi had asked.

"Films, I love films and want to make movies. I want to learn how to make them and then go to America—Hollywood!" Heinz answered. "Sounds crazy doesn't it, especially now."

"The main thing is that you get to decide about your life, not somebody else," Rudi had replied.

They had left it there until Rudi's offer came. Heinz was both nervous and excited. It felt right. The evacuation of the airfield and the order to leave for the front was ominous; he would most likely die. Here was a chance to live. All he could do was trust whatever plan the others had come up with to get them to safety.

* * * *

MARCH 31

Rudi stopped by the empty operations center. He wanted to look over the last of the weather data from a couple of days ago. Regular forecasts had ceased now that the airfield was being evacuated. Flipping through the stack of reports, he could see that the full moon was still a few days away. The days were projected to be seasonably warm followed by cool nights, which meant there would be ground fog. Good, he thought. The pattern for this time of year was holding. Rudi recalled his instructor in Hamburg explaining, "Warm air holds more water vapor than cold air. As daytime temperatures drop and the evening air cools, the water vapor falls out and condenses, such as fog."

He'd confirmed what he wanted to know; they would be able to make their move tonight with the fog giving them some cover to get away from the airfield until they had the car, as well as some moonlight for driving at night.

About to leave, he saw a leather case behind the big table. "Damn it," he said out loud. "I almost forgot the binoculars. We'll definitely need them—and the compass." Grabbing both he walked out the door.

It was lunchtime as Rudi left the operations center and made his way to Heinz's barracks. Unable to find him he figured he was already in the mess hall. There he found him sitting with Bernd, Helmut and Paul. Placing a bowl of nondescript soup on his tray with a large piece of hard cracker bread, he joined the others.

Rudi gave Heinz an expectant look and asked, "Everything in order?"

"Yes, all sorted." Heinz answered.

The others looked quizzically at Rudi and Heinz.

"Provisions," Rudi said quietly.

"Still going tonight?" Bernd asked.

Rudi nodded, "But let's finish eating and then we can talk outside."

They made small talk while they ate. Done with lunch, they stood up, returned their trays and stepped outside into the warm air. A distant droning sound made them look south toward the horizon where they could see contrails as a formation of bombers flew to their target.

"Americans," said Helmut offhand.

Standing in a circle, Paul handed out cigarettes and they smoked in silence. Rudi related his visit to the operations center and what the forecast would be. "It'll be foggy tonight with some moonlight," he told them. "Seems like the ideal time to leave."

"Where do we meet?" Helmut asked.

"What do you think about the warehouse? It's where

Ernst usually parks his truck. We can stash our gear inside until we're ready," said Paul.

"I like it, can't think of a better place," agreed Rudi. "We should have our gear there around 2300 hours, say. Ernst usually leaves just after midnight. Paul, you'll be riding in the cab, so we'll throw your gear in the back."

Paul shook his head, "Better I keep some of it. If I tell Ernst I'll be in town overnight I should have some gear with me. It'll look strange if I'm empty-handed. I can take some in a small satchel. You take the rest and the Schmeissers."

Bernd turned to Paul, "How are you going to get him to let you off before the depot?"

"I'll tell him to let me off at the Wien Gasthaus. It's fairly close to the garage that you say has a car for us."

"Is that the one with the bordello in the back?" asked Heinz.

Everyone looked at Heinz, who blushed and said, "That's the rumor I heard from one of your mechanics, Bernd."

"Then it's true!" laughed Bernd as did the others. "We know it too since we celebrated Helmut's birthday at the Gasthaus last year. We almost had to kidnap him to get him there."

"That's the point actually," Paul grinned. "Ernst will buy it, I hope."

"Paul, as a last resort you could tell him you need to relieve yourself and just walk away," Helmut suggested. "We'll just need a minute to jump out the back with our gear."

"I'll have to play it by ear," said Paul.

"Any more questions or ideas?" asked Rudi. "If not, we'll leave things as they are, hide our gear in the warehouse and meet there before midnight. Tonight's fog is lucky; it'll help us leave unnoticed. Let's hope our luck keeps up, we'll need it!"

* * * *

From a distance Paul saw Ernst's truck pull in next to the warehouse. That's odd he's early, thought Paul. To his dismay he could see someone else in the truck and realized that Franz, another driver, had come with him. They'd forgotten that the two often came together. Franz was much younger than Ernst and had served in Italy before being wounded and assigned to the transportation company at the depot. He was Ernst's muscle when it came to heavy loads.

The group's gear hadn't been hidden in the warehouse yet; now it would be harder. What to do? He decided to find out why they'd come early and walked toward the truck. In the twilight and with the ground fog starting, he had to walk right up to the truck for Ernst to see him.

"Hello Ernst, you're early for a change."

"Hello Paul, how are you? Yes, change of direction tonight. Because the airfield is being evacuated we are to take blankets, food rations, and whatever's left in the warehouse to the depot in town. Volkssturm units there need it apparently," Ernst said.

"Everything is needed to ensure victory," Franz chimed in.

Damn! With that comment Paul guessed that Franz was one of those who believed the war could still be won—a holdout. The group knew Ernst wasn't a fanatic; for him the war was like the weather, something to contend with. Having fought in the first one, he'd seen the destruction it brought and realized that the only worthwhile goal was survival. Paul imagined that he simply tolerated Franz. If only Ernst had come alone tonight; but they couldn't have anticipated this course of events. The evacuation had turned all routines on their head.

Paul simply grunted, "If you catch me in the canteen before you go, schnapps is on me. I'll leave you to it."

With a wave of his hand he turned and headed for Rudi's barracks. Shit! They would need to come up with another way to get to town. Franz would be a problem if they were found hiding in the back of the truck, and there would be no way to get Ernst to stop before the depot. But that didn't matter now; with the truck fully loaded there would be no room for them anyway.

Walking toward the mess hall he saw Bernd leaving with Heinz, having finished dinner. Paul increased his pace and caught up with them, calling out Bernd's name.

Bernd saw the look on Paul's face and asked, "What is it?"

Paul pulled them both over to the edge of the lane to let people pass and to make sure they were out of earshot, and told them about the truck.

"Damn," hissed Bernd. "We better find Rudi and tell him. Helmut is still at headquarters and will probably be working late."

"OK, you find Rudi," said Paul. "I need to eat something and will be along shortly."

* * * *

Later that evening the four of them sat quietly in Rudi's room waiting for Helmut. As soon as Rudi had heard what Paul had seen, he had sent Heinz to the headquarters building. "Tell Helmut to come as soon as he can. Mention there's a change in plans. Also avoid running into any of the SS. A truckload of people left for the front earlier this evening. The evacuation is going slowly, I think too slow for them and they might start just scooping people up."

With their plan thwarted, Bernd again brought up the idea of going to get the car and driving it back to the airfield. He'd also half-heartedly said he was ready to take the truck at gunpoint as well.

"What about stealing the commander's car?" Bernd suggested. "I can easily hotwire it and we'd be off."

Rudi was adamant that they stick together and thought that taking the truck by force or stealing the commander's car would create new problems.

By the time Helmut arrived, Rudi knew what they had to do. "Our only option is to leave by bicycle. We can make it to the edge of town by taking the forest lanes. There's an apple orchard there with a barn. I know, because that's where I first met Anna. Unless something has changed, both the barn and house are deserted. We can hide our gear there, go to the garage and then come back for it once we have the car. It's the only way I think. My gut tells me we still have to leave tonight."

The group sat quietly for a moment. "Alright, sounds feasible. But it'll be foggy and dark, we'll barely be able to see our hands in front of our faces," said Bernd.

Rudi nodded, "That's true, it'll be slower going than usual, but it won't be that bad. I'll lead; if we ride in single file you should be able to see the person in front of you. The ground fog won't be that thick, and there'll be some moonlight."

Helmut held up his hand, "I don't have a bicycle and neither does Heinz."

"No problem," said Bernd. "There are bicycles at the maintenance hangar. My mechanics use them to go back and forth between the tool shed and the field whenever an aircraft is stuck out there; beats walking back and forth. There are also some rucksacks there. They were left by those paratroopers who passed through here last year. We can leave from the hangar since it's on the south side of the airfield and close to a lane that connects to the main one in the forest."

"Then that's it," asserted Rudi. "Collect your gear and we'll meet at the maintenance hangar at midnight. If you're delayed for any reason, try your best to get to the apple orchard. If our gear is still there we haven't come back yet with the car, so just wait there. If we're gone, you could come back here before you're missed, or head south. In either case I can only wish you luck—questions?"

"Yes," said Paul. "Have anymore schnapps left?"

"Ah, I do," answered Rudi as he pulled out the bottle and placed it on the table, while Helmut passed around the glasses. Raising their glasses in a silent toast, Paul could feel his hand trembling slightly. Like the others, he knew it was now or never that they were gambling their lives.

* * * *

Rudi and Heinz arrived at the hangar with their bicycles shortly before midnight and found Bernd already there. He was on his knees stuffing his gear into one of the rucksacks on the ground. Heinz had his gear in a bundle strapped to his shoulders. Bernd handed Heinz one of the rucksacks. "Here, this will be better," he said quietly.

They waited without talking. In the distance they could hear the constant drone of muffled noises from the barracks and the occasional noise of an engine. The SS trucks or Ernst leaving, thought Rudi. The crunching sound of gravel caught their attention and they saw two figures come out of the gloom. It was Paul and Helmut. Bernd handed them both rucksacks. Talking quietly, they each secured their gear the best they could.

Paul watched Bernd coil what looked like a short piece of garden hose, "What's that for?" he asked.

"Siphon gas from the cars at the garage and when we're underway. We'll need to find some along the way as well," Bernd answered and pointed to a rolled up bundle. "That's from one of the camouflage nets we use to cover the aircraft; I cut a piece out to throw over the car whenever we stop, hopefully disguising it."

"Ah, I see," said Helmut. "That's good thinking."

"Sometimes I do," Bernd chuckled.

Rudi turned to the group, "Looks like we're ready. If it gets too hard to see we'll walk the bicycles. It'll take longer, but we can still make it before daylight."

Packed and ready to go, they all quietly shook hands. There's no turning back now, thought Rudi, I hope that we all make it.

* * * *

It was late in the evening when Colonel Steiner made it home. Quietly closing the front door he took off is hat, hung it on the coat rack and placed his briefcase on the end table. Clara, his wife, came from the kitchen to greet him.

Giving him a hug, she said, "You look tired, my dear. How was your day?"

"I am tired; I spent all day signing orders that will send people to the front, and it won't make any difference. How are the boys? Sleeping?"

"Yes," Clara answered. "They played in the living room until they dropped asleep on the carpet. They looked so peaceful. I had a time getting them up and into their beds. Are you hungry? I made some goulash with horse meat and baked some bread to go with it."

"Oh, that sounds good," sighed Steiner. "Today was busy. I only had a lunch tray sent over from the mess hall."

He sat down at the kitchen table and began to eat. Clara put a kettle on the stove to make him tea. They had been together a long time, and she knew when to leave him alone. When he first came home from headquarters, she could tell when he was still ruminating about something at work. Eventually, he'd put it aside in his mind and he'd be at home with her and their grandchildren.

When the tea was ready Clara poured it into a cup, placed it next to his bowl, and went to the living room to resume knitting scarves for the boys. This is something their mother would be doing if she'd lived, thought Clara. It had been a shock to get the news. Their daughter had been at work when she was caught in a bombing raid. They'd immediately gone and picked up the boys when they heard. Holding the knitting in her lap she looked up and wondered how their son was doing; no word from the Red Cross, so much unknown. She had no idea what America was like, but at least he was safe as a POW, away from all the destruction and this horrible war.

Steiner stared at his tea cup for a long moment, his thoughts returning to earlier in the day when Helmut had brought him that last stack of orders. He'd noticed the similarity in a few of the orders, but at first had thought nothing of it. Three from the weather group, the head mechanic and Helmut himself. Helmut was always very precise and organized, rarely made mistakes. That's why he was the head clerk, and so it was odd that those orders were missing the same information.

Ah! he thought to himself. Rudi! That's it, you're behind this. When Rudi had first arrived at the airfield in '44 to lead the weather group, Steiner had gone over his personnel file. He saw he was a competent weather technician and had a high number of flight hours. Most of them in the Arctic, which is no playground, that's for sure, he'd said to himself. He has my respect. I would know.

His personnel file included notes from his merchant marine days and previous commanders, each lauding his abilities and experience, but also criticizing a tendency to do things his own way.

Not a trait the military prefers, of course, Steiner had thought at the time. But then one has to consider that Rudi had entered the Luftwaffe as an older man with a great deal of life experience, not some malleable teenager. That fact was underscored when he found the military court order from Copenhagen regarding an incident with the use of a lethal weapon and a ruling of self-defense. Well, well, he'd thought that's interesting, probably information he'd rather be kept confidential I'm sure.

"So, you clever bastard Rudi! I think you instigated this group to pull off something," Steiner said out loud, "and I can guess why."

In '43 he'd begun to have his own doubts that Germany could win the war. As a pilot he knew the importance of air superiority and the Luftwaffe was beginning to lose it, including not producing enough fighters. Take the

Heinkel 110; a good aircraft, developed in the 1930s as a bomber and designed to be faster than any fighter plane around at that time. That changed as the Allies caught up not only with aircraft that could outperform the 110; they manufactured more aircraft and at a faster rate. There had been strategic mistakes along the way, and over time Luftwaffe losses became harder to replace, especially experienced pilots. As the world's first operational jet fighter, the Me-262 was effective and might have made a difference. But who knows, he thought. Either way it had come too late.

Steiner had kept his doubts to himself knowing they'd be problematic and only shared them with Clara. He sighed, I loved flying and did my duty.

Now what's next? he asked himself. As the airfield's commander he knew the SS wouldn't force him to the front. He planned to stay at home and wait for the British. He'd given Clara money for the inevitable day when he became a prisoner of war. It was impossible to know how long he'd be a POW. At least in the meantime Clara and the boys could stay at the house. After that, we'll see how it goes, he thought.

Well, good luck to them, easy to guess what they're doing, he said to himself. I might have done the same if I were in their shoes. Steiner stood up, placed the bowl and tea cup in the sink and went to the living room to be with Clara.

* * * *

Following Rudi, the group at first walked their bicycles until they arrived at the main lane that led south all the way through the forest to town. It was quiet except for the sound of gravel crunching under the bicycle tires. As they rode slowly but steadily, they could hear the drone of an air raid in the distance. They made good time and were close to apple orchard when they heard a sound coming their way. Rudi stopped and they all listened. Whatever it was, it came from a large engine—a truck? Coming up the lane? Rudi turned to Bernd who had been behind him and whispered loudly, "Get into the woods!"

Quickly pushing their bicycles into the bushes, they stood quietly as the sound grew louder. Everyone held their breath, hearts pounding, expecting a vehicle to pass by, but then the sound moved above them, growing into a crescendo. It was an airplane. In the gloom it passed right over them, one of its engines sputtering and sparks clearly visible. A B-17 bomber, probably damaged in the raid they'd heard earlier. As suddenly as it had appeared it was gone, maybe to crash somewhere towards the north. Relieved, the group stepped out of the forest and resumed riding south. They soon reached the edge of the forest, and ahead of them was the apple orchard. They could just see the silhouette of the barn's roof in the moonlight, the lower part obscured by the ground fog.

They gathered together. Rudi turned to Paul, "You and I will go and check out the barn. Bring one of the

Schmeissers." He told the others to move the bicycles into the woods until they were back. If things went wrong, he left it for everyone to make up their own mind what to do.

Paul inserted a clip in the machine pistol, and Rudi pulled out his Luger. They cocked their weapons and quietly walked toward the barn. Carefully they moved to the front, trying to see through a gap in the siding. There was no light, just the faint smell of apples and earth. Rudi held a finger to his lips. They stood for awhile quietly listening for any sound. There was only the rustle of something moving in the grass, probably a weasel.

Rudi turned to Paul and whispered, "Get the others; I'll stay and open the doors."

Stepping inside, Rudi moved around slowly. Moonlight shone in from holes in the roof, lighting up motes of dust floating in the air. Against one wall were stacks of ladders and on the other wooden baskets. All the tools needed to pick and collect apples, he thought to himself. Satisfied there was enough room for their gear and bicycles, he returned to the door and waited.

He could hear them approaching, the crunch of gravel and the occasional rattle of a fender on one of the bicycles. No need to fix it now, he thought. Don't need them after this. Once the others had filed in and dropped their rucksacks they stood together.

"Listen," said Rudi. "At first I'd thought that, once here, Bernd and I would go for the car, and that everyone else waits here. But now I think it's not a good idea. It's best to leave our gear here and walk to the garage together. If something comes up, we can do without the gear, but the car is essential. What does everyone think?"

"Why not just take the rucksacks?" asked Heinz.

"We can move better without them if we have to make a run for it," answered Paul. "It'd be easier to take them and not risk having to come back here, but they'd slow us down if we got into a jam."

"I'm fine with it," Bernd, interrupted. "We should get going; it's getting close to 0300, the best time to do this. The garage is not far away."

"Fine with me," agreed Helmut.

Now that they'd come this far they were all a bit anxious, but they knew that more challenges were ahead. Bernd picked up his hose and pulled a crowbar out of his rucksack. "I'll need this," he said, more to himself than the others. He slung one of the Schmeissers over his shoulder with Paul taking the other one. They filed out of the barn following Bernd.

The town was dark and quiet. The fog was not as thick here as it'd been in the forest, allowing them to see down the street. They kept close to the buildings as they made their way single file, turning one corner, then another. Finally Bernd stopped. Ahead was the garage. They stood in the shadow of the building next door. Bernd stood for a long time to see if anyone was inside until Rudi tapped him on the shoulder.

"Still good?" he whispered.

"I think so," said Bernd quietly. "The Opel's gone, must have been picked up. The Mercedes is still there. I'll try it first before the DKW. Hope it starts, it's been sitting awhile. Let's go to the side; it's dark there and then you can help me break in."

They moved quietly to the side of the garage, standing between the building and the Mercedes. Bernd lifted the crowbar to the door lock, jammed it behind the latch and waited. It was shortly going to be 0300 and the church bells would chime, covering up the sound of the latch being ripped off. They had one chance to break it while the bells chimed; otherwise, in the quiet it would be impossible to hide the sound. Bernd began to sweat as he waited. He could hear the others breathing as if they were a pack of dogs. Then the bells rang, he leaned is body into the crowbar and the latch began to release. Repositioning the crowbar he levered it again; this time the latch fell off and landed with a clank on the ground. They stood stock still, as the last sounds of the bell faded away.

"Stay here," Bernd whispered and slowly opened the door, just enough to squeeze his body through. He remembered from previous visits how it creaked when opened all the way. More than once he'd helped Horst close up and afterwards gone for a beer or dinner at his house. Once inside Bernd pulled out his flashlight, a small box type with a leather strap that could be fastened to a button on your shirt if you needed to keep your hands free. Ever the mechanic, he'd brought a second flashlight in case the batteries ran out in the first one. That one was relatively new, very compact, and didn't require batteries to operate. Almost palm sized, it had a lever that when squeezed operated a small dynamo inside, generating enough electricity to power the light bulb.

He shone the light low on the floor to keep it from reaching the windows and to avoid bumping into something and making a noise. He quickly found the hooks with the keys. Grabbing the key for the Mercedes he decided at the last moment to take the one for the DKW as well. He squeezed back out of the door, went to the Mercedes, and unlocked it.

"Stay there," Bernd told the others. "Rudi, help me open the hood."

Bernd told him to keep some light pressure on the hood so that it didn't release suddenly and make the usual metallic thump. Bernd leaned in on the driver's side and under the dash pulled the release lever. The hood lifted slightly. Rudi pushed it up and held it up as Bernd looked at the engine.

"As I thought," he whispered to Rudi. "The battery is disconnected. Simple to do in case someone tries to drive off without checking." He reattached the battery leads, turned the nuts with his hand, tightening them as best he could.

"Let the hood down, but don't latch it, makes too much noise, we can do it later," Bernd whispered. "I think we should roll the car into the street. In case it doesn't start with the key, we'll need to push start it."

"You're the mechanic," whispered Rudi. But as he was about to tell the others to begin pushing they heard the sound of a motor. It was coming in their direction, the sound reverberating off the old buildings on the narrow street.

Bernd grabbed Rudi and pulled him back into the shadows. To the others he whispered "Behind the garage, follow me!" Ducking down they moved quickly to the rear of the garage. Rudi made sure the Schmeisser was ready. Low to the ground, he peeked out and saw that the engine noise came from a motorcycle with a sidecar. He couldn't see the driver very well, but as it got nearer there was a glint of metal in the moonlight and he was able to see a flat curved metal crest on the chest of the passenger, telling him immediately they were military field police.

"Feldgendermerie," whispered Rudi to Paul.

"Shit!" was all Paul could say. He remembered them from the Eastern Front. Both the Wehrmacht and SS had military field police—easily identified by the metal crest or gorget that hung on a chain around their necks. They had a variety of roles in policing the rear area behind the front; from directing traffic, to apprehending deserters and hunting partisans. As the war dragged on they played a bigger role in searching for deserters, many who landed in penal battalions, if not executed on the spot. They had a lot of power and often acted brutally and with little cause. As a result, they were disliked by the ordinary Wehrmacht soldier.

Paul and the others knew that they had several enemies to contend with: the Allies, mainly in the form of a fighter plane catching them driving out in the open, or surprising an Allied patrol and getting shot. Their direct threat for the time being was the military field police, as well as the SS—either one would shoot or hang them on the spot for desertion.

Paul had discussed it with Rudi back in December when they'd first decided they needed to find a way to surrender, if not to the British then to the Americans. That night, Rudi had told him what had transpired in Copenhagen. Maybe it was the schnapps, but in telling Paul, Rudi seemed to want to relieve some of the burden he felt for shooting the two SS soldiers. Not that he felt especially guilty about it, he was defending himself and it was clearly either him or them. No, it was because it had been so senseless and unnecessary. Rudi had added he was lucky that the military police that arrested him were from the Wehrmacht and not the SS.

Rudi told him, "If they'd been from the SS I might not have made it to the jail, you know." He then made a fist and said, "I'm prepared to shoot if we come across a checkpoint or some other problem. We each have to face up to that possibility."

The motorcycle continued on, the sound of its motor dwindling until finally gone. "Do you think there are others?" asked Helmut quietly.

"I hope not," said Bernd. "So let's get going. Before we get the car started we'll need to get more gas, hopefully there's some in the DKW. I have to go back into the garage to get the gas cans."

Returning with two cans, he took the gas cap off the DKW and inserted the hose he'd brought. He was able to siphon off enough to fill one of the cans. He quietly put both cans and the hose in the trunk of the Mercedes, pushing the lid down gently so it only made a soft click. Then he put the key for the DKW on the front seat.

"Alright, let's see what we've got," muttered Bernd. As the others stood outside, Bernd slipped into the driver's seat. Taking a quick glance at the gas gauge, he could see the tank had gas, about a quarter full. He inserted the key and gave it a turn; the motor made a tired groan and stopped.

"The battery is run down, we'll have to start it on compression and hope it turns over," he whispered. Releasing the hand brake, he stuck his head out of the window of the car, "Start pushing."

They gathered behind the car and pushed it past the garage. Bernd steered it out into the street. Bernd waited as they pushed the car down the street until it had the necessary speed, turned the ignition key to the on position, put it in gear and let out the clutch. The car shuddered, shuddered once more and the motor started.

Quite smooth actually, Bernd thought. When everyone ran up to the car, Rudi motioned Paul to sit on the left side in the back seat with his Schmeisser; Rudi would be on the right side up front with Bernd. That way they could cover both sides.

Rudi turned to Paul, "If we run into the field police on the motorcycle and they try to stop us, the moment they stop we get out too and let them have it. We can't give them a chance to shoot first. Clear?"

"All clear, Rudi," Paul nodded, but thinking to himself that he'd never shot anyone before.

Rudi handed his Luger to Helmut, "Just in case," he said.

With everyone in the car, Bernd put it in gear and they slowly drove off. No one said a word. Under other circumstances they would have let out a cheer. They were simply relieved they'd made it this far and finally had a car; so essential to their plan.

* * * *

Arriving at the apple orchard Bernd parked close to the barn. He got out the camouflage netting, unrolled it, and asked Paul to help him cover the car. On the eastern horizon it was getting lighter; soon the sun would be up and burn off the fog. They would have to spend the day in the barn until nightfall.

Rudi could tell their adrenaline was wearing off, and they were hungry and thirsty as a result. It had been quite a night. "Let's eat something and get some rest," he suggested. "I'll take first watch. Helmut, set up the radio and I'll listen in." Turning to Heinz he asked, "What sorts of things did you get from the mess hall?"

Heinz reached for the pillow cases and started pulling out food. "Let me see, there is the bread of course and tins of liverwurst and chicken by the looks of it. I also brought two canteens of water, but they won't last long for five of us," his voice trailed off.

"That's good enough, you did well," said Paul. "We should eat our fill rather than trying to stretch out the food, keeps us in better shape. We'll find more along the way."

They gradually grew silent, each finding a place to lie down, eating and lost in their thoughts. After stringing up the antenna for the radio, Helmut sat down on some burlap sacks and ate his share of the food. It felt strange not being at headquarters, he thought to himself. He wondered if his staff and Steiner would miss him. Certainly Steiner would now know that he was making a run for it.

* * * *

April 1

Outside the barn the world was gradually waking up. Rudi sat by the gap in the siding with the Schmeisser in his lap and yawned. After awhile he pulled the binoculars out of their case and began watching the road on the other side of the orchard. Overhead, he could hear the drone of bombers; the Americans were coming in ever-increasing numbers. He knew that they had resources that Germany could no longer match, if it ever did; the Allies had an endless supply of everything. He turned the binoculars skyward to see the B-17 bombers, and watched as a lone Me-109 moved in to try to shoot one of them down. Not like in the beginning, he thought to himself. The Luftwaffe could field dozens to take on the bombers, but they were lost along with the most experienced pilots, and now there's no fuel either.

He watched the fighter strafe one of the bombers before being hit, but the pilot managed to get out and he saw the parachute open. Lucky dog, he said to himself. Putting down the binoculars he picked up the radio headset and placed it over his ears, searching for any radio station he could find.

Through the static, Rudi could faintly hear the BBC signal. It was garbled, the rising sun beginning to interfere with the signal, but he thought he heard that the Americans were on the verge of capturing Frankfurt and near Heidelberg as well. Helmut will want to know, he said to himself, Tutti is still in Heidelberg. Once the Americans are there he'll rest easier knowing the war is over for her at least.

He thought of Anna and wondered if she'd already left the airfield. Just as he was hoping that she'd made it home, he heard a crunching sound. It came from the lane where the forest ended. His heart raced for a moment as he turned the binoculars to where the lane met the street. In the gathering light saw two older men on bicycles heading into the forest, likely farmers heading to their fields, as some lived in town. He hung the headphones on a peg and stood up to walk to where Bernd was sleeping. Rudi shook him awake and, after telling him what he'd just seen and heard, gathered some burlap sacks and laid down to sleep.

Bernd took up the same position, scanning the orchard and nearby lane. As long as no one approached the barn they were safe. It grew lighter; the rising sun began to burn off the remaining fog, making it possible to see the edge of the town and people going about their daily routines.

As Bernd thought about it, they'd been lucky with the car. It figures that Horst would try the old trick of disconnecting the battery. He should have taken it into the shop. I hope you don't get into difficulties over the car, my friend. Maybe when the war is over I'll bring it back.

He stretched and let out a sigh, Ah well, what can you do? Our need was greater. And our next need is gas; one can is not enough, but it'll get us away from here at least.

At noon Paul took his turn at the gap. Bernd handed him the binoculars and to get something to eat. Paul leaned the Schmeisser against the barn door and with the binoculars scanned the edge of town. Suddenly, there in the distance he saw two military field policemen, maybe the same ones from last night, sitting on their motorcycle at an intersection as if waiting for something. Startled, Paul turned and whispered, "Hey! Bernd come and see this."

Chewing on a piece of bread, Bernd got up and walked over to the door. Just then they heard the low rumble of engines nearing. Coming into view were two trucks led by a Kübelwagen in which sat the SS captain from the airfield. The military police directed the small convoy down a specific street in town, then mounted their motorcycle and raced after it to lead the convoy in the right direction. As the trucks made their turn, Paul could see there were people in the back; it looked like personnel from the airfield.

Paul handed the binoculars to Bernd who managed to just catch sight of the last truck before it disappeared down the street. "Damn!" We got out in time then. Those bastards armed whomever they could get and now they're taking them to the front; that direction is east."

They stood in silence for awhile. Hearing Rudi get up, Bernd wave him over and they told him what they'd seen.

"Pretty much what we expected," Rudi said softly, knowing what awaited those in the trucks. "But we have our own fate to worry about. Get the others up. We have to do a few things before we leave tonight; one of them is to practice what we'll do at the checkpoints."

After Heinz and Helmut were up, Bernd told them about the trucks and military police.

"Alright, give me your attention for a moment," said Rudi. "The car is out of sight from the road and lane; we should practice our moves in case we come up to a bad checkpoint. By that I mean, one where we have to fight it out with whoever is there. Here's how we'll do it."

Rudi explained that Heinz would be the driver. It looked natural for a basic airman doing the driving instead of an officer. He changed the previous night's seating positions so that now Bernd would be in the front passenger seat; Paul in the left rear seat; and Rudi would be in the right rear seat. Helmut would sit between them. Bernd would have Rudi's Luger; Rudi and Paul would have the Schmeissers. Rudi explained that when they come up to a checkpoint, Heinz would hand over their orders only if asked, but stay in the car and keep the engine running.

Rudi turned to Heinz. "If they say turn off the engine just mention there's a problem with the engine; it may not start up. Make a big deal of it."

Rudi continued, "Paul and I will get ready to exit the car depending on who we see at the checkpoint. If it's the regular police, we'll sit tight and see how it goes." He turned again to Heinz. "If there's a problem I'll say 'drive' and you hit the gas. Use your judgment in managing any obstacles."

"However, if it's manned by SS or Feldgendermerie and they insist we get out of the car, then Paul and I will get out, but remain behind the open doors, machine pistols down. Bernd, you stay in the car, but roll down the window so you can use the Luger. If they are suspicious of us, Paul and I will move to opposite sides of the road as they'll hopefully be standing near the car and we'll have them in crossfire. That way we can get the drop on them. If they're smart they won't try anything. Then Heinz drives to the other side of any barrier and we'll run after you."

"What about me?" Helmut asked.

Rudi smiled, "Helmut, you'll be our backup."

"Backup? How?" Helmut asked confused.

"The grenades," Paul said. "I figured they might come in handy. I know what Rudi is thinking. If we get into a messy shootout, we'll be running to the car. You get out of the car and throw a grenade behind us. Hopefully it'll stop them from shooting."

Helmut looked confused, "But, I've never thrown a grenade!"

Paul picked up one of the grenades and said, "Here, look, it's easy. It's just like your mother's potato masher because it looks like one."

Paul held it up and Helmut could see the cylindrical warhead like a tin can attached to a wooden handle. On the other end was a metal screw cap. Paul explained that the handle was hollow and inside was a string attached to a toggle. He unscrewed the cap and let the toggle fall out. "All you do then is yank on the toggle to light the fuse and throw it. The long handle makes it possible to throw it far. But remember, you only have about four seconds before it explodes."

Rudi turned to Helmut, "It's very natural actually; go find a stick and practice throwing it and see how far it goes. I want to make sure you can throw it far enough behind us. The rest of us will take a few minutes to practice exiting the car, so let's go outside."

Helmut found a stick and started practicing. Examining the grenade he remembered something

Marcus Aurelius had said about death; "It smiles at us and we should smile back." He sighed. I'm not sure I can do that, he thought to himself, hoping he'd never have to use it.

The others pulled the camouflage netting off and took their positions inside the car. It quickly became apparent that practicing getting out of the car was a good idea. One of the rear door handles was tricky to open and had to be held just right to open the door. Rudi and Paul quickly found that even though the machine pistols had folding stocks and were short, the sights on the barrel often caught on the door jamb or dash as they got out of the car. They established a better way to hold them, including keeping them low when they stood behind the opened doors. That way Schmeissers weren't immediately visible. Bernd practiced rolling down his window and reaching out with the Luger. On Rudi's command, "Out!" they practiced a few more times.

Back inside the barn, Rudi said, "That was good. Not a whole lot more we can do. Oh, Bernd, one more thing. Take some of those burlap sacks and cover the head and tail lights, and for the head lights, cut a slit in the sacks to make them like blackout lights. It'll give us some light. If we don't cover the headlights we'll be seen a kilometer away." Glancing at this watch, he said, "I'm hungry, let's eat something and then we can look over the map. It's a long way to Bayreuth. If we're lucky, we'll run into the Americans well before that."

The group sat on the overturned wooden apple baskets and passed the map around as they ate, everyone taking a close look at possible routes. The map had enough detail, and a general route was apparent if they drew a straight line; however, that route wasn't feasible.

The choice of the airfield at Bayreuth had been intentional. The longer the distance to reach it meant several routes were possible; and so no matter which one they took, it left the impression they were on the way to Bayreuth to anyone checking their orders. A location that was too close would have limited their options.

"Checkpoints are our immediate problem, and we want to avoid Allied fighters as well. Never know when they decide to see what's on the ground to take a shot at," noted Rudi.

Holding the map, Heinz said, "The Landstrassen or country roads would be best and we can make it quite far that way. I know the area around Braunschweig a little from when I worked on my uncle's farm one summer in Wendeburg. It's on the way that we need to take and we can skirt Celle; I chased enough of our weather balloons around here this year," drawing a circle with his finger on the map.

Tracing his finger down the map, Heinz continued, "Here, if we take this road in the direction of Hohne, then turn south along this road here to Müden and cross the Aller River," poking the map, "we eventually get close to Braunschweig. There are a few scattered small towns along the way, maybe no checkpoints."

Paul looked over his shoulder and said, "Hmm, then we'd cross the Reichsautobahn there, the one running east and west from Berlin to Hannover and Dortmund. We'd have to circumvent Braunschweig. No telling what kind of traffic we'd find on the autobahn, maybe Wehrmacht units moving east or west depending what's happening at each front. That probably means Feldgendarmerie. Shit."

"And there would also be many refugees," added Bernd. "Fleeing from the bombing in the Ruhr before it was encircled and from Berlin as the Russians close in."

They sat in silence continuing to pass around the map.

Rudi finally spoke up, "We should get going. The light is falling and we need to get out of Celle. Soon it will be dark. I like the route Heinz suggested; it looks like there are a few roads we can take to detour around any checkpoints. Past Braunschwieg we'll run into farmland and villages. Then we just have to get around the Harz Mountains."

"Listen," Bernd interrupted. "We have to be near some towns. We'll need to find gas and food. Who knows if there's anything in these places, they're nothing but tiny villages."

"You're right Bernd, but they are the safest for now," Rudi responded, "and I'm sure we'll find what we need. We'll have to take it a day at a time."

They gathered up their gear and loaded it into the car. Heinz tucked their orders into this tunic; Paul and Rudi made sure their Schmeissers were loaded and ready; Helmut laid the hand grenades on the floor and covered them with a blanket so they didn't roll around, and Bernd strapped on the holster with Rudi's Luger. Heinz pulled off the camouflage netting covering the car, stuffed it into the trunk with the rucksacks and got in the driver's seat.

No one spoke as the others took their seats. Heinz started the car and pulled out of the orchard, onto the forest lane and to the street.

* * * *

They joined what little traffic there was and slowly made their way to the edge of Celle. Hohne was not far away. No decision had been made yet if they should turn off before that.

Bernd listened to the motor as the car drove along the Landstrasse, "Sounds good, maybe a bit of lifter noise," he told the others. He'd checked the trunk before leaving and was relieved to find a basic tool kit, along with a car jack, and to his surprise the spare tire had air in it, although the tread was worn. Good enough, he thought. It'll get us out of a jam if we get a flat. Usually people neglect the damn spare when it comes to filling the other tires with air. Good man Horst, you were thorough.

There was still some light left as they neared the turnoff before Hohne. From there the map showed a series of roads that would take them to south to Müden and onwards, but none went all the way; they would have to make several turns to stay on track.

Rudi broke the silence, "I say we go on to Hohne. It's getting dark and with the fog we could get lost if we take the turnoff. Anyone see it different?" None did, and so they drove on.

As they neared Hohne, Bernd in the front seat suddenly turned to Heinz, "Pull over between the trees, right here, quickly!" Both sides of the road were lined with trees, their canopies almost covering the road.

"What is it?" asked Rudi.

"Something on the road ahead, can't tell from here," answered Bernd.

"Let's have a look," said Rudi. He pulled out the leather case with the binoculars. As soon as the car stopped he got out and held them to his eyes. Turning the focusing knob he could see two or three people standing by a shed on the side of the road. There was enough light to see they wore leather patent helmets and their uniforms were green. They didn't seem heavily armed.

"Local police," guessed Rudi as he continued to look through the binoculars. Handing them to Bernd standing next to him, "Here, have a look, what do you think?"

Bernd took a long look and finally said, "Yeah, looks like locals. No real barrier or anything. We could turn around or chance it." He turned his head to look at Rudi and the others.

"I say we go, it'll be a test, plus there's bound to be others," said Paul. "There's no barrier so we can just run it if we have to."

"Sounds good," Rudi said. "Just relax, but be ready. It could all be nothing."

Heinz pulled the car back on the road. As they neared, one of the policemen held a wand with a circle painted white with a red ring. He walked up as Heinz rolled down the window. Bernd, Paul and Rudi all rolled down their windows too, watching the policeman. He was older, heavyset, armed only with a sidearm and a baton hanging from his belt. There were two other policeman, also older looking, standing by the shed. They seemed relaxed as one smoked a cigarette.

The policeman put his hand on the door and bent down to look into the car. "Officer Schmidt at your service; I see we have our kameraden from the Luftwaffe with us tonight," he said cheerfully.

Heinz could smell alcohol on his breath. So far no request for papers or questions, he thought, feeling his heart beat faster as he asked politely, "Good evening Officer Schmidt, how can we be of service?"

"We're looking for an airman, probably an Ami. Late this afternoon a fighter plane was seen with its engine smoking, probably got hit during this morning's raid on Hannover; it crashed behind the town in one of the fields. Farmers are all worked up about it. We know the pilot survived, someone saw the parachute. So far we haven't found him, probably hiding in a barn somewhere. Everyone's all excited. Not much happens around here, you see."

"I understand," said Heinz. "Should we see something we will of course report it, we don't want the enemy on the loose!"

Officer Schmidt nodded, "Exactly!" He tapped his hand on the door thoughtfully, as if to say something else or ask why five men from the Luftwaffe were on a side road. Having answered whatever question he had in his mind to his satisfaction he added, "Reporting would be appreciated." He then launched into the story of how he became a policeman when he'd actually wanted to learn how to fly. "In the end I discovered I don't like heights!" he laughed.

"Schmidt!" called one of the other policemen. "Get them out of here; there's another car coming."

Tapping the top of the door one more time Office Schmidt stepped back and said, "Keep a look out, carry on then," and with a one finger salute waved them on.

Heinz put the car in gear and drove off. There was silence for awhile until Helmut began quietly to giggle. His nervousness turned into uncontrolled laughing, infecting the others. Finally Helmut caught his breath, "We just met the most bored policeman in the country," he said, wiping the tears from his eyes.

"Man oh man," was all Heinz could say.

It was dark as they passed through Hohne. A few kilometers past the town they saw a white sign in the shape of an arrow with black lettering pointing to the turnoff for a village in the distance. Rudi tapped Heinz on the shoulder and directed him to turn there and pull off the road. "Over there is good." He pointed to a copse of trees, their canopies lit by the moon. Heinz drove slowly off the road toward the trees.

The ground fog and darkness made it difficult to see much as the headlights gave off minimal light. The car's suspension creaked as it rolled over the uneven ground. Parking on the far side of the trees, they were hidden from the road they'd just driven. Heinz turned off the motor; it was silent except for the ticking of the engine as it cooled.

Rudi opened his door and with one leg out turned to the others, "Let's take a break here and decide what's next. I want to see if we can get something on the radio. Helmut, do you think we could get a signal here?"

"I can roll out the antenna, but it won't be very high. Only way to know is to try it," said Helmut. "Bernd, we'll need your flashlight; help me string up the antenna."

Holding the flashlight in the sleeve of his tunic, Bernd kept the beam focused downward to keep light from shining to the side that might be seen from the distance. They worked quickly to set up the radio. Helmut sat in the open door of the car, put on the headphones and gradually moved the wire over the crystal. The others waited quietly.

Paul sat on the car's fender and lit a cigarette, when he suddenly held up his hand, "Listen!" he hissed. In the distance there was a rumbling sound and soon the others heard it too. As it grew closer, "It sounds like a truck, more than one," guessed Bernd.

Looking toward the intersection, they saw several trucks slowly pass by heading south. Visible on the back of each one was the silhouette of some type of mounted gun.

"I recognize that shape, those are 3.7cm Flak cannons," Paul said, "anti-aircraft, but used on tanks too."

"They must be heading for the autobahn and then they'll turn either east or west," said Heinz.

"Hm, yes, driving at night to avoid fighters," agreed Paul.

Rudi had been standing quietly watching the row of trucks pass. "I have an idea, it's half-baked I know, but it might work," he said. "We can make some fast progress by following them until we're close to the autobahn. We'll turn off before that. It could get us through any checkpoints if there are Feldgendarmerie. They'll think we're part of the convoy."

The idea stunned the others. With no time to discuss it, they made an instinctive decision. They saw the obvious benefit as well as the risk; it was a gamble. Rudi turned to Helmut, "Pack up the radio, you can tell us what you heard when we're in the car."

As soon as the car was on the road, Heinz sped up the best he could in the dark to catch up with the trucks. Rudi said him, "Keep them in sight, but stay back unless we come to a checkpoint, then we'll have to pull closer."

The trucks drove slow but steadily through the night, passing through Müden and across the bridge over the Aller River without incident. The group followed the convoy as it trudged south, ignoring options to turn left or right until it came to the main road that would take it to Braunschweig. At that intersection was a checkpoint, barely visible ahead. Rudi told Heinz now was the time to get closer. Everyone held their breath as the convoy drew closer and closer to the checkpoint, wondering if it would stop or continue on. To their relief it kept going with Rudi encouraging Heinz to pull up close now.

Passing slowly through the checkpoint they glimpsed several military field police, parked motorcycles and a Kübelwagen next to a building with single light, which cast a dim light onto the road. A couple of the police stood to the side as the trucks passed glancing at the car as it drove by tucked in behind the last truck. Once past the checkpoint, except for Heinz who was looking in the rear-view mirror, they turned their heads to look back and see if they were being chased.

"Start dropping back," Rudi told Heinz. "Put some fog between us; it'll keep them from noticing us. They're not going to look back anyway."

As the checkpoint disappeared in the gloom behind them, they let out a collective sigh of relief. "My god!" exclaimed Helmut, "I've never been so nervous. I couldn't stop thinking this is crazy!"

"That was crazy, but we got lucky," said Paul. "I doubt we could have fought our way through that one, Rudi, too many police."

"I know, not sure what we could have done other than run the checkpoint," agreed Rudi. "Helmut, hand me one of the other grenades. If we're chased at least that might help deter anyone after us. What did you hear over the radio?"

Helmut told them that the time had been too short and the signal was weak, but seems the Amis were in Frankfurt and further west, past some place called Homberg. "There was a bit more," he said, "but it was garbled, something about the Ruhr being encircled and many prisoners taken. Maybe General Model surrendered."

"Looks like the Allies are making progress," Bernd noted. "Let's have a look at the map. This road is taking us to the autobahn and on the other side is Braunschweig; we need to get around it, right?" Taking out his flashlight, he unfolded the map to study it.

"Heinz, how are you doing?" asked Rudi.

"I'm alright, it helps I have something to do," he answered. "It was scary back there. The first checkpoint with that bored policeman had me nervous enough."

"Well, you're doing fine Heinz," Rudi said.

"Thanks. I've been watching the odometer and I'm guessing we're not far from the autobahn. We made good progress following those guys."

Bernd turned his head to the back seat and handed Rudi the map and his flashlight. "Look here," he said pointing with his finger. "We have to decide if we're going west of the Harz Mountains or the east side."

"At the rate the Americans are moving we'll probably not meet them until we are south of the Harz. I'm guessing either side works, but let's go west," said Rudi. He studied the map and saw what Bernd had seen, a turnoff to the west just before the autobahn. From there they could continue south. Tapping on Heinz's shoulder he said, "Since you know Wendeburg, look for a sign heading that way. That's the road we want."

It wasn't long before the turnoff appeared. Following the trucks had made the driving easy, but now even with the night almost over, it was still dark enough that Heinz had to watch his speed. The few kilometers to the autobahn passed quickly and ahead they could see the dark outline of a bridge.

Rudi motioned Heinz to pull over, "Let's have a look first, plus I need to piss."

Everyone got out of the car and went about relieving themselves. Rudi held up the binoculars and could see shapes moving on the autobahn. As Helmut walked up, Rudi handed him the binoculars.

"I saw horses pulling a wagon, means there are refugees on it. Luckily the road passes under it and we can continue south. It looks clear."

Handing back the binoculars, Helmut said, "I looked at the map; south of here the roads go in all different directions. We have to be careful and not drive in circles."

"I took the compass from the operations center," Rudi told him as he turned back to the car. "It'll be like being on a ship again. We'll have to navigate. I'm more worried about driving in the daytime. This is mostly flat farmland and we'll be easily seen from the air if a fighter decides to take a look at us."

Helmut shrugged, "A gamble, isn't it?'

Rudi nodded as they got back into the car.

* * * *

APRIL 3

Heinz drove slowly into Wendeburg, taking streets that avoided the center of the town. He glanced at Bernd and then Rudi and explained, "In harvest season there are many workers on the farm, but now it should only be my uncle and his wife. But to be safe I should go alone to see them. There are trees just before the farm where we can park. What do you think?"

"That works," said Rudi. "We can watch the house and see who's there."

They parked in the grove of trees. Crouching down, they moved up to the edge of the grove and lay prone on the ground. Rudi brought out the binoculars, and they took turns watching the house and the fields beyond. They could see Heinz's uncle go in and out of the barn doing chores, while his wife fed chickens in a coop. Suddenly another man came out of the house wearing a coat and hat like he was about to leave.

"Heinz, who is that?" asked Bernd, handing him the binoculars.

"Damn!" muttered Heinz. "Not good; he's the foreman when workers come for the harvest. I know for sure he's a committed party member. Hard to say why he's there now—might have been bombed out in town and was assigned to live there."

They watched as the man pushed a bicycle up the driveway to the road, mounted it and started pedaling toward Braunschweig.

Rudi turned to Heinz, "Well, we've watched long enough. There's likely no one there other than your aunt and uncle. No way to know how long the foreman will be gone. Go and see them. Give us a wave if it's safe. Should something go wrong run this way and we'll provide cover. Ask if they can spare some food."

"And gas," added Bernd.

As the others continued to watch, Heinz approached the farm. Bernd went back to the car and opened the trunk. Taking out the full gas can, he poured it into the tank. Rudi walked over, "How are we on gas?"

Holding the can, Bernd tipped his head and looked at Rudi, "Could be better. At the apple orchard the gas gauge read a quarter tank, assuming the gauge is working correctly. With this, it should be close to half full. To reach Bayreuth we'll need more."

"Hm, alright," nodded Rudi. "We'll have to steal some."

Bernd chuckled, "Rudi, this war is turning us into thieves."

As they talked, Helmut ran over. "Heinz waved us to come," he said.

Bernd got in the driver's seat and slowly backed the car out of the grove. The others got in and they drove toward the farm. Heinz was standing in the courtyard with his aunt and uncle, watching them drive in.

Rudi was taken back to his days on the farm as he walked up to Heinz's uncle. They look just like the farmers from home, he thought. Their faces were brown with the permanent tan from working outside and their hands were rough. Heinz's aunt wore an apron with a print of tiny flowers faded from use, and the uncle, in his boots and suspenders holding up patched pants, reminded him of his father.

Heinz introduced them, "This is my Uncle Ralf and Aunt Marie."

"Nice to meet you," said Ralf, shaking their hands. "Well, you better pull the car next to the barn and come inside. You can't stay long; Herbert will return this evening. He works in town."

Once all were seated inside, Marie placed bread and cheese on the kitchen table. "I'll make some tea," she said, to which the group murmured their appreciation. Standing by the stove as the water heated up, she turned to them. "You know, I almost didn't recognize Heinz when he first walked up. I thought 'who is this man?' maybe a refugee. We get them coming by every now and then."

"More and more actually," said Ralf. "We see the bombers flying overhead and that means more refugees come, pulling wagons with what they could save or carry on their backs."

The group ate in silence as Heinz told his aunt and uncle what he had been doing for the past year at the airfield, and how he enjoyed working in the weather section. Then he told them why he was wearing an airman's uniform.

His uncle wasn't surprised. "The moment I saw you, it was my first guess," he confided. He turned to

Rudi, "I was in the first war you know, saw nothing but death and still ask myself what was it for? It was all just meaningless slogans; never got a real answer. Lots of young men tried to get out of the war back then, some even went to Switzerland and sat it out there."

Rudi nodded, "My father was in the first one too, and so were all the fathers of my friends when I was growing up."

"Hmm," Ralf said, stroking his chin, "you've probably read Remarque's book?"

"Yes, All Quiet on Western Front was very popular," answered Rudi. "I wanted to see the film, but it was banned almost right away, so never got to see it."

"Well, the book got it right, because Remarque was there. You'd think after everything that happened during and after that war, nobody would want another," asserted Ralf.

"No one expected or wanted one," offered Paul. "My father was in the first as well. Once everyone was able to find work after the Depression and the economy improved, people were comfortable; many didn't take the slogans seriously, not realizing the danger."

The conversation continued in that vein, until Marie said, "Ralf, that's enough talk about the war; these boys have to get going. I wish we could have you stay, but Herbert was a Blockhelfer, assistant to the neighborhood warden when he lived in town. We heard that he reported people for the slightest thing. We also have a family staying in your old room, Heinz.

Nice people with two small children. They're in town seeing the doctor; the girl has a fever, probably chicken pox or something."

"You're right my dear," Ralf replied. "Put some food together for them to take. Bernd is it? You wanted gas. Come with me. I don't want Herbert to notice that there's less of it without some reason, so I can't give you much."

Bernd stood up and followed Ralf to the barn, telling him, "We're grateful for whatever you can spare."

Outside they started to say their goodbyes. Ralf called Heinz over to the side. "Here," handing Heinz a revolver. "It was my father's when he was in the Navy in the 1890s. It's old but it works. These are the only bullets I have for it."

Surprised, Heinz said, "Thanks!" taking the revolver and the handful of bullets. The revolver was heavy. He saw that the wooden grip was worn, as was the bluing.

"Listen, only put five bullets in at a time, so that the chamber behind the hammer is empty; that's the 'safety' otherwise it could go off by accident. I hope you won't need it. Don't worry about returning it. The Americans will take it from you anyway, and I have another one. Come and visit us after the war is over. I know you have your heart set on making movies, more than shooting people," Ralf said with a wry smile.

He clapped Heinz on the back, and they walked over to the car. Once everyone was seated, Heinz started the car and with a short wave slowly drove down the driveway. In the rear view mirror he saw his uncle and aunt watching them leave, standing with their arms around each other. He turned south onto the road, and they disappeared from view.

* * * *

It was daunting to look at the map, given the distance they'd need to cover, should they have to go all the way to the airfield at Bayreuth-Blindlach. They guessed it was close to 400 kilometers, requiring them to swing around the Harz Mountains. In normal times it would be a long day's drive. Back at the farm, Ralf had suggested they just hide somewhere until the Americans came; it would only be a matter of time. Rudi had agreed, but felt that if they were discovered they could find themselves trapped and have to fight their way out. Being mobile gave them choices, and they could adjust their plan based on what they heard over the radio and maybe surrender earlier.

Heading south to skirt Braunschweig, they drove one back road after another. At crossroads that weren't on the map, Rudi used the compass to direct Heinz which way to turn, keeping them moving in a southward direction. On the way, they passed the occasional car, a tractor, groups of refugees, and even Wehrmacht soldiers on motorcycles who were most likely messengers. Now they might see more traffic and likely a checkpoint.

Rudi tapped Bernd on the shoulder, "The binoculars are on the floor; use them occasionally to look in front of us." To Heinz he said, "Turn here, we need to go east a bit before we head south again."

They caught up to a truck with workers in the back. "Probably working on the autobahn," guessed Heinz.

"Stay behind them," instructed Rudi.

Eventually, the road neared the intersection where the main road went south to Goslar and the Harz Mountains. They hoped to take it south, but turn off well before Goslar and the Harz. It was a better road and they could drive fast for a stretch before driving again on side roads.

Bernd grunted, "Something up ahead. Better pull over and let's have a closer look." Taking turns looking through the binoculars, they could see it was another checkpoint. It had a permanent look about it. Across each lane of the road was a bar painted with red, black, and white stripes that was raised to let a vehicle pass through. Sandbags were stacked high along the roadside, and parked to one side was a scout vehicle with a machine gun. There were two lines going each direction. The best they could tell, one appeared to be for civilians, the other for everything else, probably military and locals. The distance made it hard to see exactly, but the military side looked like it was being managed by regular police, while the civilian side was by the Feldgendarmerie.

"My bet is the Feldgendarmerie are looking for deserters among the civilians, only reason they'd pay attention to them," said Paul. "The police are just checking papers."

As they debated what to do, a motorcycle with a side car and two Wehrmacht soldiers passed them. Watching it, Rudi said, "I think we should chance it. We'd have to backtrack to find another way to get to the highway and there might be a checkpoint there as well. Let's get behind that motorcycle; the lane will be clear once it's through. We can run it if we have to. That bar doesn't completely reach across the road. I think the car will just fit through that gap. Then we'd have to drive like hell before they turn the machine gun on us."

Rudi turned to Paul, "Here, take the hand grenade. Can't shoot our way through, but a good distraction would help, so keep your window rolled down. Drop it when I tell you, but only when we're past the bar."

"I'm so tense!" confessed Helmut. "But I believe that we can make it. This is taking years off of my life."

The others laughed nervously. They'd been lucky so far. Turning onto the road, they drove up behind the motorcycle just as the policeman handed the riders back their papers, waving them forward at the same time. Passing the civilian line next to them, they saw it was long in both directions. There was a mix of local workers on bicycles and refugees, some pulling a bollerwagen filled with their belongings.

The policeman bent down to look at Heinz and said, "Your papers."

Heinz pulled them out of his tunic and handed them over. He had placed his uncle's revolver under his thigh so it was easy to reach. The others had covered the Schmeissers and the grenades with blankets on the floor.

The policeman studied their orders, "Ah, being transferred to Bayreuth. Now that's a long way, even for the Luftwaffe." He didn't seem particularly suspicious, but wanted to know more. He began asking each one what work they did at the airfield, all the while looking at their orders and nodding occasionally.

Seeing that Rudi and Paul were officers, he was about to ask them something, when there was sudden commotion and loud shouting in the civilian line. Two Feldgendarmerie were wrestling with a man in civilian clothes they'd identified as a suspected deserter. In the struggle the man was getting the better of them; it was clear he was experienced in close-quarter fighting and about to get loose, but with two more Feldgendarmerie running to help it would be to no avail.

The policeman watched the man being led off behind the sandbags and turned back to them, "Poor bastard, they'll shoot him or send him to a punishment battalion to fight the Russians."

Bending down, he looked at them silently for a moment and then slowly handed the papers to Heinz without a word. Stepping back, he waved them through and signaled the car behind them to pull up. The policeman standing at the bar pushed down on the counterweight, raising it. Heinz put the car in gear and they drove through. The mood was solemn in the car as they contemplated what would happen to the man.

Eventually Bernd spoke up, "Probably an infantryman who's had enough of the war."

"He knew how to fight," said Paul. "If they send him back to the front I think he's the type that will survive no matter what. At least I'd like to think that."

* * * *

Heinz turned the car southward onto the main road and accelerated.

Running his finger down the map, Rudi told the group, "We don't want to go all the way to Ringelheim. Let's turn off at this small town here. There we have choices to drive side roads as long as we angle southwest."

The discussion to stay on the better road until it split—one side going to Goslar, the other west—had been brief. The experience at the last checkpoint had been sobering, making the choice to stay on rural roads for the time being an easy one. At the same time, the incident had also hardened their resolve to fight it out should it come down to that.

Speeding along, they caught up with a small convoy of trucks covered with branches to camouflage them from the air.

After following them at their slower speed for awhile, Bernd finally told Heinz, "Just pass them."

Heinz pulled out briefly to see down the road then hit the gas and the Mercedes accelerated past the trucks.

Passing the truck at the rear of the convoy they could see it carried wooden cases, probably ammunition; the next two were filled with soldiers sitting in rows. The country was wide open and soon the convoy slowly receded behind them.

Suddenly, Paul who'd been looking out his window gasped, "Look! To the left! There's an airplane!" In the distance they could see a low-flying airplane. They recognized it as a fighter plane. It had been flying opposite their direction, but now it slowly made a gradual turn. The pilot had seen them.

"Shit, it's coming our way!" stammered Helmut.

There was no cover as the plane made a low approach straight at them. Rudi felt calm, but knew that Heinz, being young, might panic. Under duress it can be hard to hear and one's field of vision narrows. He'd have to give him clear and simple commands.

Rudi leaned forward in the back seat close to Heinz, "Listen to me! When I tap you on the shoulder, brake hard. When I tap you again, speed up. We'll keep doing it and hope we can throw his aim off."

Watching intently as the plane drew near, Rudi waited until it was close enough to shoot. He tapped Heinz on the shoulder and yelled, "Now!" Heinz hit the brakes throwing them all forward in their seats. When Rudi tapped Heinz again he immediately accelerated, the low gear making the engine scream as they picked up speed.

Rudi tapped him again, "Hard brake!"

The pilot let loose a short burst of machine gun fire,

but it hit well in front of the car. Rather than come around again, the pilot adjusted his path with another turn to target bigger game—the convoy. This time its machine guns struck the last truck. The plane continued to fly west until it was a dot on the horizon.

Looking out the rear window, in the distance they could hear explosions and see smoke coming from the last truck as the ammunition cooked off. The other trucks had pulled forward and stopped.

"The pilot probably thought we were part of the convoy," said Paul.

"He's not coming back," said Helmut, almost hopefully.

"Maybe low on fuel?" guessed Heinz in a shaky voice. He'd seen the plane at the same time that Paul had. Fear had shot through him and it'd taken all his concentration not to lose control of the car. It had helped having Rudi tell him what to do.

"Could be or out of ammunition; they don't carry that much," said Rudi.

Seeing Heinz's pale face, Bernd turned to him and in a calm voice said, "He's gone now. Probably finished escorting bombers somewhere and was looking for ground targets on the way back. You can slow down now; at this speed we're using too much gas."

The fast driving had brought them to the turn off at Lobmachtersen sooner than expected. From there they resumed driving by map and compass, zigzagging their way in a southwest direction, passing little villages, fields, and rows of trees planted as wind breaks.

"I need to stop and take a break," announced Heinz as he pulled the car over next to a row of trees. They all got out and stood silently looking around. They could smell the fresh fields; the sinking sun cast a golden light on everything, including their faces. Paul lit a cigarette and passed around the pack and his lighter. They smoked in silence, recalling the man at the checkpoint and the attack on the convoy.

Finally Helmut cleared his throat and asked, "Why not go straight to the Harz and stay in the forest, away from these open areas?"

Sitting on the car's fender, Rudi turned to Bernd next to him. "Do you want to tell them what you heard?" he asked.

Bernd nodded, and leaning his arm on the roof of the car, turned to the others. "We want to stay away from the Harz. It's been awhile, maybe a few months, but do you remember the paratroopers who were at the airfield, the ones who left the rucksacks? Well, they were being transferred to the Harz, the south side somewhere. The short of it is, there's a buildup there to keep fighting, using the Harz Mountains and the dense forest. If we drive too close we'll definitely run across hard-liners and holdouts who want to fight to the last man. We'd be forced into their crazy plans and if we refuse, it'd be bad for us—either way."

Glancing at Rudi, he gave a nod of his head, "Your turn."

Rudi cleared his throat, "Alright. Well, in early '44 I went on leave before being transferred to Hustedt to visit my parents and sisters. One thing I wanted to do was get them to understand they may have to evacuate west and to prepare for it. My parents wouldn't have it. My father in his best Platt Deutsch insisted he was staying; can't blame him. Our family has been there since around the 1700s. That makes the idea of leaving shattering, I suppose. My sisters took me seriously at least. Anyway, while there I ran into an old friend, Walter, from my school days. He was the smartest of all my friends growing up and had left the village to become an engineer."

Rudi cleared his throat again, "Walter told me he'd worked at some facility in Peenemünde, which is up the coast from my village on Usedom. All very secret, something to do with the wonder weapons we keep hearing about. Pretty much figured out he worked on the V-2 rockets by the sounds of it. The British bombed the place heavily, so production was moved to a town south of the Harz. I think one reason he told me all that is because he was disturbed by what he saw there. He told me the forced laborers that built the factory and the rockets live in very bad conditions. Didn't say more, just shut up suddenly; probably realizing he might have said too much. I told him not to worry, I wouldn't say anything."

"But what does that mean for us?" asked Heinz.

"It's dangerous for us there," Rudi said. "It means there's lots of security and SS around such a facility. Maybe the whole area, who knows? So we have to keep some distance from the Harz, the south at least; probably the west side too."

The others were silent, absorbing what they'd heard. They continued to stand by the car, each lost in their thoughts until Bernd said, "Getting close to sundown. We should move on and find somewhere for the night."

As they drove off, on the horizon to the east they could see the foothills of the Harz, and towards the north high up in the sky, the contrails of bombers flying to their target.

"Berlin," murmured Paul.

Coming to a sharp curve in the road, Heinz slowed the car. After the road straightened, he exclaimed, "Hey, look!"

Drawing closer they saw it was a truck, front down in a ditch on the opposite side of the road. Probably the driver had taken the curve too fast and couldn't correct in time.

Bernd told Heinz to slow way down and stop next to the truck. The cab was empty. It was abandoned. "Nobody in it; let's check it for gas," declared Bernd.

"I thought you'd say that," chuckled Rudi.

Bernd motioned Heinz to pull in front of the truck and stay in the car, but keep the motor running. He stepped out and opened the trunk taking out the gas cans and hose. Paul and Helmut stayed with Heinz, while Rudi went with Bernd carrying the Schmeisser. It was getting dusk. Not likely the driver would return, but if he did and there was gas in the truck, they were determined to take it no matter what.

Bernd tapped on the tank, "There's gas, could be a can's worth."

"Make it fast," urged Rudi. "We're exposed here."

"I am, I am, it'll only go as fast as gravity will allow," muttered Bernd.

They stood in silence, Rudi looking up and down the road as the gas slowly poured into the first can and then the next. The way the truck leaned made it hard to completely fill the cans, leaving Bernd with two cans each half full. When he'd finished, Bernd replaced the caps on the gas tank and both cans. They jogged back to the car, placing the cans and hose in the trunk.

"Let's get going!" Bernd said excitedly, "I feel better!" He felt responsible for keeping the car going and was relieved they'd found some gas. Watching the odometer and gas gauge, he'd calculated how much they were using and knew they were close to running out. At least for now they had enough, and he could relax.

Not long after leaving the abandoned truck, a dim light appeared on the road ahead, coming their way. As the light grew nearer they saw it was an old truck with its blackout lights on and three people sitting in the front. As they passed each other the driver briefly turned his head to look at them, but kept going.

Bernd laughed and slapped his knee, "Hah, farmers! I bet they're on their way to pull the truck out after all. At least there's a small amount of gas left in the tank and it'll start; I couldn't get it all out. They'll think they have plenty and then run out somewhere and figure we took it."

Even in the failing light it was possible to see the landscape begin to change. There were flat, open farm fields to the right, but increasingly on the left were clumps of forest rising up to the hills in the far distance. The long drive and the events of the past days had everyone tired. Helmut dozed in the back seat, while the others struggled to keep their eyes open.

"I'm tired, we're all tired, we need to sleep somewhere even if it's in the car," sighed Rudi. "Watch for a place to pull off."

They drove for another half hour, thinking it might have to be the car. Then in a field by a row of trees they saw a small hay barn. Bernd told Heinz to stop the car at the roadside, while he checked out the barn. Walking up, he looked in and waved them over. Driving slowly off the road, the car creaking as it rolled over the field, Heinz pulled up to the structure. Haying season wouldn't be until the summer; the hay that had been stored here was from last year and that had been mostly used up. Heinz was about to pull the car inside, to hide it from the road, when Rudi waved him off and told him, "Back in; it'll be better if we need to leave in a hurry."

Stepping out of the car, Heinz thought there's not much hay left. Hope that means the farmer won't turn up.

They pulled out blankets and coats, making small piles of hay to sleep on. Rudi asked, "Who wants to take first watch?"

"I'll take it," offered Helmut. "I had a short nap in the car."

"We leave before sunrise," said Rudi as the others

settled in. "And Helmut, we should try the radio tomorrow before we leave."

* * * *

April 4

It was still dark when Paul woke Rudi and told him, "Sunup is an hour away."

Rudi sighed and slowly stood up, brushing hay off his uniform. He folded his blanket and walked over to the car; taking out one of the canteens, he splashed water on this face and took a swig. Turning to Paul, he asked quietly, "How was the night?"

"Quiet, except for the damn mice running around here. I'm guessing Magdeburg got bombed; you could see the flashes reflecting off the cloud cover."

Rudi yawned, "Alright, I'll wake up the others. Is there any bread left?"

"Some, in the pillow case," Paul said. "There's a tin I opened that has some jam left."

Gradually everyone began to stir. Helmut sighed, "What I would give for a cup of coffee and a wash up." Looking at the others he noted, "You know, we need to find some water, we all need a shave, we're looking pretty rough."

"I'll buy you a cup of real coffee when the war is over. Yes, a shave would feel good," Bernd said. "Let's set up the antenna and check the radio. Anyone look outside yet to see what's around us?" He turned to Heinz. "Go ahead and take the binoculars, but don't be seen."

Helmut strung the antenna across the barn and set up the radio, put on the headphones and began to listen. At first he could only hear static, until finally capturing a radio signal. Listening intently for while, he took off the headphones, "The Americans are in Kassel and might be approaching Mühlhausen. That's all I could get."

Rudi nodded, "Last week they were around Marburg if I remember correctly. That means they've made around 100 kilometers since, so they're moving fast. You know, we might find them this week if they keep it up. Let's get ready; it'll be light soon. Bernd, do we need to add that gas from last night?"

Bernd ducked into the car and turned the ignition key, looking at the gauge, "I'll add one of the cans so we'll have an empty one in case we find more."

Heinz walked into the barn, saying he hadn't seen much. A farmer, with horse and wagon, had passed by, and he thought in the distance he could see people probably refugees on the main road. He handed the binoculars to Bernd, got into the driver's seat, and started the car as the others took their seats. Driving slowly across the field and onto the road he turned the car to the west.

* * * *

They made their way past small towns, the rural countryside giving no sign that there was a war. Here and there farmers were out in their fields. "Must be getting ready for planting," said Heinz.

Ahead, the road would eventually reach a point where several roads intersected. Having just circled around the town of Elbe, they discussed the likelihood of a checkpoint there. The more they drove west and the nearer they came to the front, checkpoints would be more likely.

Bernd said, "Let's pull over, I want to look at the map."

Rudi leaned forward and held up the map so that Bernd and Heinz in the front seat could see it and said, "Look, my thinking is this; we cross the main road below this town," pointing at it on the map. "Then we duck under this town here and turn southwest on this road that goes all the way to Alfeld. That way we swing wide of the Harz and whatever is going on there. This area is mostly farmland, but there are trees if we need to hide."

"Hm, after that it gets woodsy alright," said Paul, "right up to the Weser River. But we won't get across; bet the Wehrmacht has blown most of the bridges by now."

Rudi nodded, "I agree, but we don't need to cross the river. At the river we wait for the Americans, if they aren't there already. Even they didn't know what kind of progress they'd make once they crossed the Rhine. They've gone faster than I thought, and with this pace they could be at the Weser this week. The British are already past the river in the north."

They discussed their limited options, until Helmut pointed out, "There's no way to know what's best, other than to go there and adjust if we need to. I'm for the

Weser. Tonight we may know more. What we need is to find food."

To that the group murmured their agreement.

As they drove, Paul asked, "How much money does everyone have? Since we don't have ration cards it'll be hard to get food—if any is even available."

Bernd was sure they could buy food from a farmer or the black market. He described how one of his mechanics at the airfield wanted eggs, but since they were rarely available in the mess hall, he went searching for them. Somehow he managed to do a deal with a local farmer.

"We let him cook them in the shop because he shared them with us at least. He was probably trading some of our tools for the eggs," chuckled Bernd. "Anyway, our best option is to buy food from a farmer or the black market."

The flat farm fields gave way to the forest. As they passed through, Helmut noticed a stream paralleling the road. It wasn't hard to convince the others to stop and wash up. Turning off the road, they drove up the next lane, finding a place to park. They piled out of the car and began taking off their tunics. At the streams edge was a pool.

Rudi said, "Its perfect, but we need to take turns watching the lane; I'll go first."

Watching them wash, Rudi could see that they looked pretty bad; unshaven and unkempt from sleeping rough gave them the look of what they were; desperate men on the run. It was good timing to clean up; they'd be less suspicious. They passed around the one bar of soap they had and a razor. When Paul was finished, he walked over to Rudi and told him to take his turn.

Rudi handed him the Schmeisser and said, "You look much better Paul, hardly recognize you!"

"Yeah, yeah, if you could see yourself," smiled Paul. "It feels good to wash up."

The last to finish, Rudi was buttoning up his tunic when they heard sounds coming from the lane. Walking slowing toward them was an elderly couple leading a cow. Farmers, thought Rudi. He motioned for Paul to hide the Schmeisser. The man and woman stopped when they saw the group standing around the car.

Helmut waved and greeted them, "Good day to you."

"And good day to you," the old man responded. As they walked closer the woman asked, "Are you lost?"

"No, we stopped to rest and wash up," said Helmut. The couple didn't seem interested in why they were there; the man grunted and began pulling on the cow's halter to get it moving again.

"That's a healthy cow; are you moving her between fields?" Rudi asked the man.

"That's right," he answered.

Rudi told the man about growing up on a farm and the fishery. They chatted back and forth about living and working on a farm. The man said, "On a farm you learn what work is!" To which Rudi agreed.

Paul interrupted and asked, "I'm wondering if you could help us? We are looking for food. If you have any to spare, we can pay."

The man had warmed up talking to Rudi and paused, looked in the distance for a moment, then at the woman, and then back at them and said, "We can sell you some rabbit, smoked it myself. We raise rabbits now since there's not much meat available these days. We don't have much of anything else; have to wait until the garden produces. Come by our farm; it's not far away, next road to the right."

The woman chimed in and told them that stores in the villages and town of Alfeld didn't have much food either; with long lines they often ran out of food before some customers could reach the counter. Looking at her husband she said, "There is one store that always seems to have something."

The man grunted, "That's true, who knows where they get it; worth trying if you can pay."

He went on, "You have to go to the rear of the store after closing time. You might get lucky, but swatch out—they're black market gangsters." He encouraged the cow to move and they walked on, with the woman occasionally slapping the cow's haunches.

"What does everyone think?" Bernd asked when the man and woman were gone. After some back and forth, they decided to get the rabbit since it was on their way. All of them had eaten it before. Rabbits were easy to raise, including in the city were they made up for the meager meat ration. At the start of the war rationing had been minimal and had been supplemented by food from the occupied countries.

Now, shortages had become extreme, and rationing foodstuffs had increased.

Driving slowly they caught up with the couple as they turned into the driveway of their farm. The man led the cow into the barn. After awhile he came out with a package of rabbit meat wrapped in newspaper. As Helmut handed him the Reichsmarks he'd demanded, the woman came out with a small bucket of milk and a ladle offering them each a drink.

So delicious," said Bernd.

She handed them a couple potatoes and pointed to their well, "Take some water too."

The man watched them prepare to leave. "Our son is in the Luftwaffe too, in Normandy. From what we know he's a prisoner of the British there. At least he's safe. I assume you are trying to do the same?"

Rudi looked at the man and nodded.

"Well then, I wish you much luck," the man said.

They got in the car and drove off. Once on the road, Heinz turned his head to Rudi in the back, "Are we going to that place in Alfeld?"

"Yes. It seems like our best chance to find some food," answered Rudi.

* * * *

Arriving at the outskirts of Alfeld they hid on a rise in the forest on the north side of the town, which lay below. With the binoculars they scanned what they could see of it. A fair amount of refugees were moving through it, and occasionally a truck covered in branches rolled through to the west.

"Refugees fleeing east," observed Helmut, "might mean the front is close."

While waiting for evening and the store to close they shared the rabbit. They cooked the potatoes over a small fire in one of the empty tins from the airfield mess hall. For five people it wasn't enough, the little bit of food only making everyone hungrier. Sitting on the ground they waited and watched the road.

Finally Rudi stood up, "It's time, gentlemen. I'll need all your Reichsmarks, no telling what prices will be." After handing over what they had, everyone got into the car.

The farmer's directions had been good and they quickly found the store. They drove by it to get an idea of what the area was like. An alley to the side of the building across from the store looked like a good spot to park out of sight.

Rudi turned to the others and said, "Paul and I will go to the store. Heinz, Helmut you two stay with the car. Bernd, I'll need my Luger for awhile, but leave the holster in the car. Take the Schmeisser instead and follow us, but hang back and just keep an eye on the back of the store. I'm pretty sure we'll have to go inside. Things could go easy in there or they might make it difficult. I have a good idea who these people are; I saw plenty of them when I was at sea. We might have to come out fast; in that case a shot or two in the air should dissuade anyone after us. And because the black market is illegal, we have to watch for the police too."

Heinz looked at Paul through the rear-view mirror and told him, "You can use my uncle's revolver."

Paul clapped Heinz on the shoulder, "Thanks! I'll feel better having it."

They didn't have to wait long before they saw the Geschlossen sign go up. Rudi signaled them to go. Paul grabbed one of the pillow cases. Bernd wrapped his Schmeisser in one of the blankets and placed it under his arm.

Tucking their pistols in their waistbands they walked across the street. The store was on a corner with a tall row of bushes down one side broken up by a gate leading to a courtyard at the rear of the store. They went through the gate and found two other people already there waiting. The two gave them furtive glances, but said nothing. Bernd walked past the gate. It looked like there was another, more secluded way to the courtyard from the rear. After about ten minutes the door opened and a man stuck his head out. He waved the two in and told Rudi and Paul, "Wait."

A few minutes later, the door opened and the two people stepped out of the door and scrambled away with bags under their arms. The man waved them over, but stayed standing in the doorway.

"What do you want?" he asked.

"We heard that we could buy food here," Rudi answered, taking a roll of Reichsmarks out of his pocket he showed it to the man and then put it back. Before coming, Rudi had told Paul that if it's just the shopkeeper there shouldn't be any problem, but if it looked like a gang they might have to act accordingly. When the man had first opened the door Rudi had instantly pegged him as a thug.

The man said, "Wait here," and went inside closing the door.

Rudi turned to Paul, "Looks like a gang to me, the kind you find in seaports and in the bad part of town. Hard to say what they will try and pull, but we have to beat them to it, whatever it is. Be ready." Rudi turned to look at the back of the courtyard; he could barely see Bernd, who was leaning against a coal shed.

The door opened and the man waved them in. He stood in the doorway as they squeezed past him. That puts him behind us, thought Rudi.

Inside it took a moment for his eyes to adjust. There were two men sitting at a table in what looked like a storeroom. On the table was a pistol. A large, muscular man stood up. "Welcome gentlemen. I understand you are in need of some provisions. Doesn't the Luftwaffe feed its men anymore?"

"Well, we are in transit and ran out," answered Paul.

Paul glanced at the shelves filled with tins of all kinds. He recognized them as Wehrmacht rations. These people either had a deal with a corrupt supply officer or had hijacked a supply truck. Rudi was right, he thought, they're thugs alright. Probably the store up front has nothing to do with this; they're just selling contraband out of the back part. The store owner may not have had a choice in the matter.

"Hm, I see, well, look around and see what you'd like to buy and we'll tell you the price," the large man said, waving an arm at the shelves.

Rudi gave a nod to Paul who began picking up various tins and putting them on the table. When he was done, the large man told them the price. Rudi reached for the money in his pocket, all the while keeping an eye on the man sitting with the pistol in front of him. Counting out the Reichsmarks he placed them on the table and motioned for Paul to scoop the tins into the pillow case.

His hand reaching for the money, the large man turned to Rudi with a menacing grin, "You know, it's strange to have Luftwaffe personnel here. Did you know there is a reward for turning in deserters?"

"Yes," said Rudi, as he pulled the Luger from his waist band, pointed it at the head of the man sitting at the table and snatched his pistol off the table.

Paul moved to one side. Holding the pillow case in one hand, he pulled out the revolver, cocked the hammer and pointed it at the thug standing behind them to block them from reaching the door. Virtually snarling, Paul told him to move away from it. Startled, the man looked at the others and, with arms slightly held up, moved away.

Backing toward the open door, Rudi shouted at Paul, "Let's go!"

The man sitting screamed, "Dirty deserters, you're traitors to the fatherland; you deserve to be shot!"

"You deserve it more; you're war profiteers stealing from soldiers!" shouted Rudi from the doorway.

He and Paul ran through the courtyard to the gate. As Paul opened it, they heard a staccato burst of gun fire. Turning his head, Rudi saw that all three thugs had run to the door to go after them, one with a pistol in his hand. The burst from Bernd's Schmeisser had hit the door jamb above their heads, forcing them back inside

They all raced to the street. Heinz saw them crossing at a run, started the car and pulled ahead to meet them. The three were barely in the car when Paul yelled, "Drive!"

All three were panting from running and laughing at the same time. "Wow! That was close!" gasped Paul. Turning to Rudi he asked him how he knew that those men wanted to turn them in as deserters.

"Well, when you enter one of those places you have to figure you might turn out to be the commodity, because you're more valuable for whatever reason. They would have gotten money or a big favor for turning us in!" he said.

"And we'd probably be dead," muttered Paul.

* * * *

Their drive out of town was slow at times as they navigated through throngs of refugees with their wagons and carts, some pushing baby carriages filled with whatever personal belongings they could take.

Eventually, they were on a back road and heading west along the edge of the forest using the compass to determine their direction.

Since everyone wanted to eat the food they'd bought, they decided to find a safe place as soon as possible. They also needed to set up the radio to determine how close they were to the front. Just past the town, they discovered several lanes that led deep into the forest. They chose one at random, wanting to be settled before dark. Inside the forest they soon came across a stack of logs that had been harvested.

Heinz parked the car behind the stack. While the others covered the car with the camouflage netting, Paul pulled out the pillow case and dumped the cans onto the ground so that everyone could pick out what to eat.

Bernd started a small fire to heat the cans. He filled the largest empty can from the airfield mess hall with water from a canteen and dropped the smaller cans into it. He carefully placed the can on the fire, bringing the water to a boil. As long as the cans were completely submerged in water, they wouldn't explode. Soon they were all enjoying hot food.

Meanwhile, Paul helped Helmut string up the radio antenna between two trees. Sitting sideways in the front seat, Helmut put on the headphones and began to listen, while the rest waited quietly for any news. Every now and then they heard rustling sounds in the woods—alarming them—but they soon realized it was just wild pigs moving through the underbrush.

Helmut removed the headphones and told them, "It'd hard to hear, but I think the Americans are still outside of Mühlhausen, which means that they crossed the Werra River at least. Seems the fighting in Kassel is over. The garrison there put up a fight, but that didn't stop the Amis."

"If they crossed the Werra," noted Paul, "that means they are just south of us."

"If we keep going south we should run into one of their units somewhere, maybe even tomorrow," Rudi said.

* * * *

April 5

It was still dark as they quietly packed. Bernd wanted to use up the last can of gas. Since the battery in the flashlight was dead, Paul held the dynamo flashlight, squeezing the lever to provide a flickering light for Bernd as he slowly poured the gas into the car's tank. Meanwhile, Heinz made a fire to heat up the last of their canned food. As they ate, they sensed that today might be the day they had been striving for. All of them knew that approaching the Americans would be dangerous. They had the pillow cases as white flags, but would that be enough? They might be shot if they bumped into a patrol unexpectedly. Low flying planes had passed over during the night. It seemed the Americans were close.

Ready to go, they took their seats in the car and Heinz turned the ignition key. Nothing! He turned the key once more. Again nothing, "Damn it!"

Calmly Bernd told him, "Unlatch the hood; let's have a look."

Lifting the hood, Bernd used the dynamo flashlight to check the engine. The others waited quietly, the whirring of the dynamo flashlight the only sound. Bernd quickly determined the problem, a loose belt. The generator had shifted slightly in its bracket, causing the belt to loosen and slip, preventing the battery from being adequately charged.

Bernd lifted his head from under the hood and told Heinz, "Get me the tool pouch out of the trunk; it's an easy fix. But we'll have to start the car on compression."

"Good thing there are five of us," muttered Paul.

As soon as Bernd had tightened the belt and closed the hood, Heinz got in the car to steer, while the others pushed it out from behind the stack of logs and onto the lane. They began to push as fast as they could down the lane.

Bernd finally yelled, "Now!"

Turning the key on, Heinz put the car in gear and let out the clutch; the engine shuddered a moment and then started. There was an audible sigh of relief from the group as they got in and caught their breath.

In the back seat, Rudi looked over the map. "Let's head west and turn south at Holzen; we'll be on the main road a bit until we can turn off here," tapping the map with his finger. "There's a string of small towns after that and lots of back roads. Here, have a look."

The map was passed around.

"Looks workable," agreed Helmut. "It will keep us east of the forest, not many roads there."

"And once we are south of this forest, we can turn west to the Weser, right?" asked Heinz.

Bernd sitting next to him shrugged, "Looks like it, we'll see. Let's just get going."

From what they could tell, the front was getting close, making them more cautious. Heading in the direction of Wagelnstedt, the countryside became pastoral with open fields laid out on slightly rolling hills in all directions and forest in the distance. The curves meant they couldn't see what was ahead or coming their way, and so Heinz slowed the car as they rounded a curve or crested a slope. He also watched the rear view mirror for anything gaining on them. Once they saw a truck pull onto the road behind them; luckily a section of forest was nearby and they could turn off to let it pass.

"Looks like a workers' group," said Paul.

Before returning to the road, they debated their limited options: drive along the edge of the massive forest to the west, where they could hide more easily, or keep going in the general direction of Moringen, which was more direct. That meant open countryside with only the random tree grove alongside the road.

"The hell with it!" replied Bernd. "I'm for Moringen; none of the ways are necessarily safe. What we'll need soon is gas and if we can find it, food."

"That's true," said Rudi. "Alright, let's keep going then."

* * * *

Late in evening they came to a small village, the narrow cobblestone street winding its way through to the other side. Many of the buildings in the villages tended to be close to the road. Coming around a sharp bend they saw a large farm ahead. They passed the rear of the barn followed by a large arched entrance to the inner barnyard. They could see a well in the middle of the yard and a low building bordering the far side. Rudi tapped Heinz on the shoulder and pointed ahead to a tall stone water tower surrounded by trees. "See that? Look for a spot to pull over where the car won't be seen."

"What are you thinking?" asked Bernd.

"I want to watch that farm back there for awhile. There's a car in the yard, near the house. Maybe there's gas we can steal. Plus we need more food."

"They must have chickens there," Heinz chimed in. "Be easy to catch one and wring its neck."

Helmut pointed out that while having a chicken would be nice, they had no easy way to cook one and it would make a racket trying to catch it.

"Well, that's true," responded Heinz as he pulled the car off the road and parked between a row of trees and the water tower. Rudi got out of the car with the binoculars to scan the farm.

An approaching bank of clouds in the distance caught Paul's attention and he watched it for awhile. Looking at his watch, Paul turned to the others and said, "It's going to rain soon by the look of those clouds. With the wind speed and direction I'd estimate shortly after sunset."

"That would help us," Rudi said as he handed the binoculars to Bernd, "Have a look at the car and that tractor, could you siphon gas out of them? Whoever owns the farm is more than just a farmer, maybe some type of local official with a car like that."

Bernd scanned the farm and car, "Hmm, yes, some important party member I suppose. Yes, easy to siphon the gas from the car. The tractor is a maybe."

"What do you mean maybe?" asked Rudi.

"I'm not an expert on tractors, but some of them run on kerosene. The engine is started with gas and once it's warm you switch over to run on kerosene. It's cheaper. I'm not sure if it's that kind of tractor or not."

Rudi shrugged, "Ah, I see. Well, let's concentrate on the car unless we find gas in the barn.

"So you want to go into the barn too?" asked Helmut. "It's huge! It'll be hard to see anything with that simple flashlight."

"You're right," agreed Rudi. "We'll look in the milk house. On our farm, once the cows were milked, it was put in cans and stored in a cold water bath to keep it from spoiling until it's picked up. It's also a good place to store food because it's cool in there."

Paul added, "When the rain comes it'll be dark, everyone there will be inside. Be hard to see anything out of the windows."

Rudi outlined what he had in mind. Bernd and Paul would go with him to the farm. Bernd would siphon gas from the car, but pass on the tractor—too much trouble.

The gas cap on the car was on the side away from the house so Bernd could get to it unseen. At the same time, Rudi and Paul would search the milk house for food.

"It stands to reason there's food in the barn and the milk house," asserted Paul. "These farmers always make sure they have enough food for their family. But for the government quota they're supposed to deliver, they underestimate the harvest or amount of meat available. The 'difference' they sell on the black market for a good price."

"If this farmer isn't a party official, then maybe he's good at cheating the quota and black market money bought the car," reasoned Heinz.

"Could be," answered Helmut. "But buying a car now? Wouldn't go unnoticed and the village would look down on someone showing off. No, probably an official of some kind is my guess."

"It doesn't matter who he is, let's get some rest. I'll take first watch. Helmut, I'll wake you in a couple of hours," said Rudi.

* * * *

The rain came as Paul had predicted. The patter of raindrops on the roof of the car lulled them to sleep after the long day. Along with the rain came occasional claps of thunder, but no lightning. In the dark they could occasionally hear the clip-clop of horses pulling a wagon through the village, and above the overcast, every now and then the drone of airplanes; otherwise it was quiet.

Early in the morning Heinz, who had the last watch, woke everyone up. "Its two o'clock," he whispered.

It was still raining as they got ready. Bernd pulled an empty gas can and the hose from the trunk. Rudi slung the Schmeisser over his shoulder and handed Paul the Luger.

Rudi turned to Helmut, "Take the other Schmeisser. If something happens, give us some covering fire. Shoot high, in this dark it's damn hard to see anything. Hopefully scare off whoever is chasing us." Turning to Heinz, he said, "If you hear shots start the car and pull it to the side of the road, ready to go."

Heinz said he understood.

With that, the three walked across the street and up to the arched gate that led into the inner yard. They lined up against the wall of the entrance, looked inside and waited. The main house was dark, and the only the sound was the rain. Rudi waved his hand forward and they each strode to their targets. The occasional thunder was welcomed as they walked across the large open yard. Reaching the car, Bernd bent down and removed the gas cap and inserted the hose. He'd have to siphon the gas by feel in the dark as Rudi had the flashlight.

At the same time, Rudi and Paul approached the milk house door. It was unlocked and they stepped in, their nostrils filled with the familiar smell of milk and other farm odors. Squeezing the flashlight lever, they saw a wooden bar with sausage rings near the wall and shelves with small rounds of cheese. They grabbed what they could and stepped out, carefully closing the door. As they walked over to the car to see how Bernd was doing, they heard a bark.

Damn it! thought Rudi. Of course they'd have a dog, I should have known.

Walking faster, they reach Bernd, and Rudi whispered, "We have to go, now!"

"Not full yet," Bernd whispered back.

The barking continued. In a top floor window a light came on.

"No time, let's go," insisted Paul.

Pulling the hose out of the tank Bernd grabbed the can and followed Rudi and Paul to the gate. They heard the lighted window open and a man's voice call out, "Who's there?" as the dog kept barking.

There was a peal of thunder as they ran through the gate. Crossing the street, they reached the car, and Rudi told Heinz to start it. Bernd put the gas can in the trunk as Paul hurriedly dumped the cheese and sausage that he had in the trunk too. Rudi stood outside guiding Heinz as he backed the car out from their hiding place and onto the road. Before getting into the car he looked back to the farm to see if anyone had followed them; seeing nothing but rain and darkness, he got in.

As they drove off, Bernd told the others, "I didn't put the gas cap back on the car and they'll know someone was there. I think we got three quarters of a can at least."

Paul asked Heinz to turn up the heater. "I'm wet and cold," he said. "How about we stop soon, I'm hungry again. That sausage looked much better than what was in the tins."

The others murmured their agreement.

"We should stop soon anyway," said Heinz. "It's hard to see the road in the dark with this rain, and we can't tell if there's a checkpoint ahead."

After awhile they found a section of forest that hadn't been turned into a field for planting. Bernd walked ahead to guide Heinz until they found a clearing to stop. The rain began to let up as they ate some of the food from the farm.

"Wish I had some of that milk," sighed Rudi. "It smelled good in there."

Lounging in the car, they took turns describing their favorite foods. Rationing throughout the war had replaced many foods with ersatz products, and none of them tasted the same.

* * * *

April 6

Rudi suggested that they listen for any news before the sun came up. "We're close to Moringen; somewhere past there we have to turn west to the Weser River, if I remember from the map."

The radio was set up and Helmut began to listen. It took awhile, but he finally removed the headphones and sighed. "Nothing new, the fighting in Kassel is over. I couldn't make out the rest; a strong signal from another station playing classical music overlaid it."

Looking at the map, Rudi told them there was a major road past Moringen where they'd have to take a dog leg. There might be lots of traffic on it, but it would get them to the turnoff to Wesertal. They took turns studying the map.

Helmut finally said, "I'd prefer we went toward Kassel. From what I could hear, I'm guessing the Amis have crossed the Werra River and are on this side already. It's a bit farther than to Wesertal, but at least we know the Americans are there. At Wesertal we might have to wait for a long time."

They discussed his idea until finally all agreed that it was the better option. Bernd poured the gas from the farm into the car's tank.

"That's it for gas. It should be just enough, given the consumption so far," said Bernd.

"Alright then, gas will decide our destiny," quipped Paul.

They packed up and resumed driving. Past Moringen and onto the main road, they found long lines of refugees.

"Where are they going?" asked Heinz, weaving around horse drawn wagons and people pulling bollerwagen.

"Probably Göttingen, the nearest biggest city," guessed Bernd. They were silent as they drove past the refugees, each wondering how their own families were doing.

They skirted the west side of Göttingen and turned onto the road that would take them to the confluence of the Fulda and Werra rivers. They hadn't driven very far when in the distance they could see something on the road. Bernd told Heinz to pull over so they could get a better look. They got out of the car, each taking a turn with the binoculars. They could see a hut on the side of the road and stacks of sandbags, and barely visible, a white painted sign with black letters that read 'Danger! Uncontrolled area ahead, all vehicles must stop'.

Next to the hut was a motorcycle with a sidecar and a Kübelwagen. From this distance they could see five or six figures. Three of them wore the camouflage uniform used by the SS, light reflecting off metal crescents on their chests: Feldgendarmerie. It was hard to discern what the others were wearing. Paul thought they could be Volkssturm militia to help the SS.

Bernd was first to speak. Clearing his throat he said, "I hate to say it, but we might need to rely on what we practiced at the apple orchard in Celle."

"From the sign, this must be the last checkpoint before the front, before the Americans, right?" asked Paul.

"Could be, it's only a few kilometers to the river," said Helmut.

"One thing in our favor," noted Rudi. "See how the road curves sharply after the checkpoint. If they shoot at us, we'll be out of range quickly unless they decide to chase us."

Helmut asked, "Can't we go around. Maybe there's another way?"

Looking at the map, Bernd said, "Doesn't look like there are any side roads. We'd just run into another checkpoint."

"Plus, this looks like the shortest distance to the front," added Paul.

They talked through what to do. Their plan would be triggered if they were ordered to turn off the motor and step out of the car.

"Paul and I will get out. We should be able to surprise them," said Rudi.

They returned to the car and rolled down all the windows. Paul and Rudi checked the Schmeissers, each chambered a round and took off the safety. Bernd checked the Luger, holding it in his lap. In the back Helmut held his grenade and loosened the metal cap slightly.

They drove slowly down the road. Nearing the checkpoint they could see by their arm bands that the others were Volkssturm, essentially civilians with a rifle. Luckily, they didn't see any Panzerfausts, an antitank weapon that could be used on the car. But that didn't mean there wasn't one in the hut.

Stepping away from the hut, an SS soldier held up his hand and walked into the road so he would be at the driver's side of the car when it stopped. He bent down with his hand on the roof of the car as Heinz stopped.

"Your documents, and turn off the engine."

Heinz made a face and shrugged, "Ah, the motor is a problem, won't always start when it's been turned off."

The SS soldier was about to repeat turning off the engine, when a second SS soldier walking with a slight limp came over to the car and asked, "What do we have?"

"Looks to me like they're Luftwaffe," answered the first SS soldier.

The second SS soldier took one look at them and making a jerking motion with his thumb barked, "Everyone out!"

At that moment, Paul and Rudi got out of the car and walked to opposite sides of the road, aiming their Schmeissers at both SS soldiers. The look of surprise on their faces showed them that they had the drop on them.

"Heinz, drive through, slowly; we'll be behind you," ordered Rudi.

The face of the SS soldier with the limp went from surprise to fury. He turned to the Volkssturm and the third SS soldier standing by the hut and snarled, "They are deserters! Traitors! Shoot them!"

As one of the Volkssturm fumbled with the bolt on his rifle, Bernd, who was nearest, stuck his arm out of the car window with the Luger and shot twice into the hut, "Stay where you are and do not shoot!" he commanded. The three Volkssturm froze for a moment and then quickly skittered behind the hut.

Rudi and Paul slowly backed toward the car now at the far side of the checkpoint. Both kept their Schmeissers pointed at the first two SS soldiers, who stood exposed in the open road shouting insults at them, but knew that they couldn't do anything for the moment. From across the road, Paul saw the third SS soldier standing next to the hut reach for his rifle. As he brought it up to take a shot at Rudi, Paul let loose a burst from his machine pistol into the hut, showering the SS soldier with wood splinters. Paul warned him he'd shoot him with the next.

Now a fair distance from the checkpoint, Helmut got out of the car. He'd removed the cap on the grenade so the toggle on the string was dangling free. All he had to do was yank it to light the fuse. As Rudi and Paul reached the car, the two SS soldiers saw their chance to shoot and ran to take cover behind a stack of sandbags. Rudi fired a burst in their direction and yelled at Helmut to throw the grenade. Helmut yanked on the toggle and threw it as hard as he could. The two SS soldiers saw it coming and ducked down behind the sandbags. The grenade bounced twice as it landed in the middle of the road, exploding with a thump.

Rudi stepped on the running board of the car facing the checkpoint and let loose another burst from his Schmeisser. "Get in!" he yelled to Paul and Helmut as they literally dove into the slowly moving car moments before Heinz gave it gas. The car surged around the corner and the checkpoint was out of sight. Heinz stopped briefly to let Rudi get into car.

"My god!" exclaimed Helmut shakily. "I might be the first teacher of the classics to throw a hand grenade at our own soldiers."

Turning his head to look at Helmut, Bernd said, "You should include it in your curriculum vitae."

"I think I might," chuckled Helmut.

Their euphoria of having made it through the checkpoint was short-lived. All of a sudden Heinz shouted, "They're after us!"

Behind them they could see the motorcycle with both SS soldiers. The one in the sidecar gave a short burst from his Schmeisser in their direction. Rudi asked, "Where is the other hand grenade?"

"It rolled under Heinz's seat," shouted Paul, as he bent to the floor and felt around with his hand under the seat. "I got it!"

Rudi held out his hand, "Give it to me!" He told Heinz to speed up. "I want to time the grenade. If they're too close they'll just pass over it before it explodes." Unscrewing the cap, he waited for the right moment.

Meanwhile, Paul leaned his torso out the open window and fired short bursts from the Schmeisser; the shots went wild, but the motorcycle slowed a bit. With a look back, Rudi flicked the hand grenade behind the car, watching as its momentum made it bounce wildly on the road. The soldier driving the motorcycle saw the grenade and overreacted by turning so sharply that the sidecar lifted off the road with other soldier in it. The driver lost control and the motorcycle tumbled off the road into a ditch as the grenade exploded on the road.

"Damn those dogs!" exclaimed Paul. "I hope that was the last checkpoint. If not and they have a field telephone they'll call ahead and warn the next one we're coming."

Helmut felt sure that it had to be the last one. "The front is maybe only about ten kilometers away now, so there's no point for another one," he insisted. Either way they were committed and all they could do was drive on.

They slowed as they approached the small village of Dransfeld. Passing through, the village appeared empty. There was no one around, except ahead a lone figure walked toward them. It was an older man with a cane. Heinz pulled the car alongside him.

Bernd stuck his head out of the window, "Good day, where is everyone?"

The old man stopped and looked at them, "Good day to you. They evacuated."

"Why didn't you?" asked Bernd.

"Too old to care about it," said the old man.

"Do you know where the Americans are?" asked Rudi.

The old man nodded and pointed with his cane to the west. "Not far," he replied.

They wished him luck and drove on. After a few kilometers the road began to descend slightly. Helmut remarked that they might be entering a river valley so they must be getting close. As he finished his sentence, the car began to lurch.

"Ah, shit!" snapped Bernd. "We're out of gas and nothing's left in the cans."

In all the turmoil getting past the checkpoint, they hadn't paid attention to the gas gauge. Not that it would have made much difference, since they had no more gas. When the engine finally died, Bernd told Heinz to take it out of gear and let it coast, hoping the gradual slope would carry them further.

"We need to ditch the car," insisted Rudi. "We're a good target moving this slow. The river is close and we can walk there. It's probably not far. The car did its job."

After pushing the car off the road and into the trees, they packed their rucksacks. They decided to take the weapons with them until the last moment; it was still unclear what lay ahead. Bernd wrote a short note and placed it on the dash: This car is the property of Horst Auto Repair in Celle. It is functional. Out of gas. He then covered the car with the camouflage netting. He gave the hood an affectionate pat; hoisted his rucksack on his shoulder and hurried to catch up with the others. Turning in the direction of the river, they walked single file alongside the road.

* * * *

April 7

The morning sun filtered through the trees, burning off the ground fog and waking them one by one. It had been a chilly night. When they'd abandoned the car the previous day, it was close to dark, but they decided to walk through most of the night to make some distance between themselves and the checkpoint. In the middle of the night they began to hear distant noises that were hard to discern. They all agreed it was best to get some rest and wait until daylight to see what was ahead. Exhausted, they'd all fallen into a deep sleep, not even bothering to take turns keeping watch.

"Good morning, gentlemen," said Rudi. "This could be the day!"

"I'm ready for this to be over," muttered Heinz, slowly waking up.

"Don't bet on it," said Helmut. "Our odyssey continues, but in another realm, one entirely new to us, I think."

"You are so cheerful in the morning, Helmut," teased Paul. "But you're right. Being a prisoner of war will be a different matter."

"And something to survive," added Rudi. "I'm serious. We should eat what's left of the food now. Once we surrender and are amongst our comrades in arms, I suspect food will be a source of conflict. I've seen starving people in Asia fight each other over a bag of spilled rice. We're not any different."

The group absorbed his comments silently. They split what little food that was left and passed around the canteens of water.

Bernd tapped Rudi on the shoulder, "Let's you and I walk ahead and see what's up there. Bring the binoculars and the Schmeisser."

Rudi grunted in acknowledgment.

While the others waited, Bernd and Rudi walked up the road for about an hour to where the road made a steep drop down into a valley. From the crest of the hill they overlooked a huge field that extended to the banks of the Werra River. In the field below they could see a mass of soldiers sitting or standing in groups, their voices reaching them like a constant murmur.

The sight had them both speechless.

"There must be thousands down there!" Bernd finally said.

Rudi held up the binoculars and scanned the mass of soldiers, "Mmm, looks like they're Wehrmacht. But I don't see any Ami soldiers; they must be on the other side."

Scanning downriver he saw a damaged railroad bridge. Whether it had been bombed by the Allies or blown up by the retreating Wehrmacht, the metal bridge had remained somewhat intact. It still spanned the river; except it leaned precariously on its side, sagging in the middle just at the water line. He could see soldiers crossing to the other side by gingerly climbing and sometimes crawling, over the twisted metal beams.

Rudi handed the binoculars to Bernd, "Here, have a look. That's what we're in for."

Silently Bernd scanned the mass of soldiers below them. "None of them have weapons that I can see. There seems to be a group of officers in charge at the bridge lining up groups and sending them over," he said.

"That's where we want to be when we get down there," said Rudi, pointing to the group of officers. "We don't want to stay on this side for any length of time. Food is on the other side, not here. It could take a long time to get this many across."

"I see what you're saying; at least we know which direction to move. Most down there are probably waiting to be told what to do," said Bernd.

Rudi handed the Schmeisser to Bernd and told him to stay out of sight while he walked back to get the others. A couple of hours later Bernd heard the group approaching. They took turns with the binoculars scanning the area below them. It was an astonishing sight as they stood there in silence. Finally Helmut said, "So this is what surrender looks like."

Rudi thought for a moment, "Yes, and we need to survive it too. Let's stay together and get to the bridge so we can get over as soon as possible. There's a trail through the forest over there that parallels the river. If we follow it before making our way down, we'll end up closer to the bridge."

The trail eventually took them down a steep slope and to the crowd of soldiers nearest the bridge. Other than a glance, hardly anyone noticed them. Passing a group of Wehrmacht officers, one looked over and recognized their Luftwaffe uniforms and realized that they were armed and called out to them, "New here I see!" Pointing at the officers behind him, "We're in charge of managing troops until they are across. You must clear your weapons and turn them in—only unarmed groups are allowed to cross."

The group learned that the commander of his regiment, what was left of it, had contacted the Americans to arrange surrender. They were going over in groups and would be met by the Americans on the other side and searched. He didn't know what would happen after that.

Bernd asked him where to dispose of their weapons. The officer pointed, "That way, you can't miss it. There's a pile."

His instructions took them in the direction of the damaged bridge. Slowly they wended their way through the crowd of soldiers. Some had bandages from wounds and sat in carts that their comrades had pulled to get them here, others were wrapped in blankets looking ill. Bicycles were strewn about as well as more carts. The sound of hundreds of shuffling feet and the steady murmur of everyone quietly talking was occasionally punctuated by a groan from a wounded soldier.

When Rudi found the pile of weapons, he pulled the clip from the Schmeisser and pulled back the bolt to clear it. As he placed it on the pile, he suddenly felt naked. Well, he thought, I must have gotten used to it. He watched as Bernd cleared the other Schmeisser and added it to the pile.

Bernd then handed the Luger to Rudi and said, "It's yours."

Rudi nodded, remembering how it had saved his life once. He cleared it and laid it on the pile. Turning to Heinz, he asked about the revolver. Heinz told him he'd left it in the car.

"Wish I could've returned it to my uncle," he sighed.

"Your uncle would rather have you back," said Helmut.

The group continued to edge their way toward the bridge. As they got closer, the crowd became more densely packed; the process to send groups over was slow. They waited, moving up inches at a time, like entering a crowded theatre. The day wore on until it became dusk, and crossing would be too dangerous. They would have to wait until the next day.

They sat silently among the soldiers. Occasionally someone asked about their home towns, trying to find someone from home, or shared the latest rumor, of which there were plenty. No one talked about the war or where they'd been; they'd all known it, and there was nothing left to say. Except all wondered what would happen next. As it got darker, the huge crowd began to bed down the best they could. The night would be chilly, and not all would wake up in the morning.

* * * *

April 8

The sun was just below the horizon, casting strands of light high up into the sky as Rudi woke up. Leaning over, he shook Bernd who was curled into a ball and quietly snoring. He wanted the group to be ready to move as soon as people were allowed to cross the bridge. Yesterday they had witnessed two soldiers slip and fall into the river. One managed to pull himself back onto the bridge, but the other had been swept downstream by the current, his head bobbing above the water until he disappeared.

Bernd had whispered to Rudi, "Kind of shitty to die just as the war is over for you."

Rudi had given a small shrug and nodded. What could you say?

As it grew lighter, the rustle of soldiers waking moved through the crowd like a wave. Bernd woke up the others and they shuffled closer to the bridge. Given how many were ahead of them, they were assured of making the crossing that day.

Then Helmut, with his head close to Rudi whispered, "I can't swim."

Momentarily startled, Rudi looked at Helmut and quietly assured him, "You can do it. We'll help you. Empty your rucksack and give it to me. It can throw you off balance; without it you can move better. I'll be next to you."

Helmut nodded, "Thanks." The contents of Helmut's rucksack were divided among the others. Rudi tied the empty rucksack to his.

The officer at the bridge told them that fifty would go at a time. Once they were across, the next fifty. "No crowding or pushing! Don't stop, just keep moving!" he repeated to each group.

The soldiers were disciplined and the process was orderly. The group moved up with the others, and soon it was their turn to cross. Bernd went first and then Rudi, followed by Helmut, Heinz and Paul. Climbing across took concentration. Walking on the metal beams sometimes required having to side step to reach the next beam while searching for the next hand hold. It took time, but they couldn't stop with others behind them.

Helmut had one bad moment in the middle where the rushing water line was just under their feet. Behind him Heinz encouraged Helmut to not look down, to do one thing at a time and just find the next step.

Reaching the other side of the river, Rudi and the others expected to see American soldiers, but none were visible. They followed the others on a path that had been trampled into the grass leading to a tree line in front of them. There they saw a large group of American soldiers. One of them separated himself from the group and in perfect German told them to line up and drop their rucksacks or anything else they were carrying at their feet. Other American soldiers walked over and began to methodically search them and their gear. Not far away stood armed soldiers looking relaxed, but watchful. Anything that could be a weapon was confiscated, but they were allowed to keep blankets and clothing and personal items. The German-speaking soldier ordered them to fall into formation, four to a row; and then along with several guards, marched them to the other side of the trees.

There the Americans had turned a large farm field into a makeshift POW camp by surrounding it with barbed wire. The field was divided into sections and was full of soldiers as far as the eye could see. Not far from the camp was a village, which was close enough that it was possible to see the inhabitants walking about.

At the entrance, Rudi and the others were surprised to hear that managing the camp had been turned over to the Wehrmacht, with the Americans only providing oversight. A consequence of so many soldiers surrendering that their captors were overwhelmed.

Walking through the gate, they looked for a spot to settle. Bernd told the others that they might be better off near the edge of the camp, closer to the wire fence on the village side. It quickly became obvious who had been here awhile, as they'd dug pits and constructed makeshift shelters using their blankets and coats.

As they settled near one of these groups, a ragged-looking soldier walked over to them and asked, "Do you have anything to eat? We've been here a week and only once had some soup and bread. We've been making soup from grass and weeds."

"No, nothing," answered Helmut. "We've been on the run for days and ate everything we had."

The man nodded and shrugged. He introduced himself as Georg, from Dresden, and told them, "If you want water, the Amis run hoses into the camp near the gate. Don't drink too much, it's very chlorinated and gives some of us diarrhea. With so many here, the latrines are cesspools, so shit somewhere else. If you get any food, don't let anyone see it, they'll try to take it from you."

"Do you know what they're going to do with us, Georg?" asked Bernd.

Georg shrugged, "Rumor is they'll transport us to a transit camp to be processed, but no one knows when. They released most of the Volkssturm—old men and kids in the Hitler Youth; disarmed them and told them to go home. The Amis have their hands full with so many of us. When the guards are distracted sometimes the villagers throw food over the wire. Everyone fights for it like dogs." He paused for a moment and warned, "No one knows what's next, but whatever it is, you have to survive here first," and walked back to his group.

Looking around, the five took stock of their situation. There was a kitchen facility near the gate, but it hardly seemed up to the task of feeding the many soldiers here, and no medical services were visible; the wounded sat out in the open with the others. It was apparent that the sheer number of soldiers surrendering in such a short time had taxed the ability of the Americans to find enough food and shelter for them all.

Paul leaned over to Rudi, "I think this is a potato field," he whispered. "Might be some strays."

Rudi nodded, "Could be, if they haven't been found already."

Helmut, returning from the latrines, sat down next to them, "I'm more worried about getting sick. Georg over there was right, the latrines are over filled, definitely shit somewhere else."

The afternoon turned into evening, and they tried sleeping the best they could.

* * * *

April 9th

In the morning, they woke to the sight of a body being removed on a litter; someone hadn't made it through the night. It had been cold and they felt stiff and hungry. One by one they wandered off to relieve themselves. Throughout the morning more prisoners arrived. Around noon they noticed that the prisoners sitting around them were watching the village intently. Walking from the village toward the camp was a group of women, maybe two dozen, pulling several bollerwagen. The sight of the women caused a stir among the prisoners.

Bernd walked over to where Georg was standing and asked, "What's going on with those women?"

Not taking his eyes off the women, Georg told him, "Hah, you're in luck. The Americans have those women cook food for the camp; different groups go to the other end. If we're lucky we'll get some soup and bread. We haven't seen them for a few days. Take it from me; be ready to move up when they order us to stand in lines. You want to be near the front; last time they ran out."

As the women arrived at the camp, an American military truck pulled up, backing up to the camp's kitchen area. Several American soldiers jumped out from the rear of the truck and began unloading boxes filled with what looked like bread, while the others stood guard with their rifles, wary of anyone coming near.

Rudi watched as the women unloaded the bollerwagen filled with potatoes and what looked like heads of winter cabbage. They quickly chopped up both, throwing everything into several large vats, then added water and placed vats on metal racks over a fire. The American soldiers stacked the loaves of bread onto a litter to carry into the kitchen area where the women cut them into slices and piled them on a table.

The mass of soldiers began to slowly creep toward the kitchen area. One of the Wehrmacht officers shouted orders to form lines; each line would be served from one of the vats. Standing next to the officer stood several Feldgendarmerie to make sure order was kept. Rudi and the others moved up to join one of the lines.

Standing in line, Paul nudged Rudi and whispered. "See that Feldgendarmerie on the far right? I'm pretty sure he was at the last roadblock."

Rudi gave a low chuckle, "I think you're right. Nothing he can do now, eh?"

Once the soup was ready, the line began to slowly move. Luckily, they still had their mess kits. The women ladled the soup out as fast as they could, while others handed out a slice of bread to each prisoner, which most began to eat as they walked away; while the Wehrmacht officer shouted at everyone, "Move! Keep moving!"

Rudi and the others returned to their place where he suggested, "Maybe we should save half of the bread for later. We don't know when we'll eat again."

"It will be hard to not eat it. I'm still hungry," groaned Heinz.

Finishing his soup, Helmut said, "That tasted wonderful!"

It was not enough, but they all agreed that the simple soup had been delicious, mainly because they were so hungry. Paul lit a cigarette, took a long draw and then passed it around to the others. Next to staying healthy, confronting the boredom of waiting and the uncertainty of what would happen to them would be a challenge.

* * * *

APRIL 15

It had been overcast for days and it had rained again during the night, keeping the field muddy. The group was miserable; they'd only had soup and bread one other time since arriving at the camp. That morning they witnessed a fight over some potatoes thrown over the barbed wire by an old woman from the village. One of the guards chastised her for causing a disturbance. She had made a 'so what' gesture with her hand as she turned to walk back to the village and said to the guard, "There's nothing you could do to me at my age after all I've lived through. I feel bad for the boys."

The potatoes hadn't landed near them, and so all they could do was watch as a fight broke out. Rudi was sure he heard someone in the melee growl in an effort to get a potato. Turning to Bernd who was bundled in a blanket, he muttered, "Hunger is bringing out the animal in us, isn't it?" Bernd shrugged, feeling too miserable to rely.

Helmut, sitting wrapped in his blanket and staring blankly at the horizon, had overheard Rudi. He recalled what Marcus Aurelius had said about human lives being brief and trivial. The war, this place, has made life trivial, yet we'll do our utmost to live. It's worn me down, but I refuse to die in this place, he said to himself.

They'd been worried about Heinz, who'd been coughing and suffering from diarrhea for a couple of days now. At first they thought it might be cholera as there had been an outbreak in the camp with several deaths. Their worry eased when Heinz's symptoms didn't worsen and he seemed to be improving.

Georg walked over in the afternoon to share the latest rumor with them, "The Americans are going to move us for processing soon. Some transit camp that used to hold Allied POWs and is now empty."

Among all the rumors that circulated, some bizarre, this one sounded hopeful. Still, all they could do was wait. Bits of news from the outside drifted in as well. Some prisoners volunteered for work details to get extra rations. The details were overseen by American soldiers, and the prisoners would overhear what progress was being made on the front. The latest was that the Americans had reached the Elbe in the east and encircled the Harz, where there was intense fighting—confirming Bernd and Rudi's concern that it was to be avoided.

* * * *

April 20

Georg's rumor finally came true. That evening they received word that their section of the camp would leave the next day for a transit camp south of Kassel that had held Allied POWs during the war. The group began to feel optimistic. Heinz was recovering, but still weak; the others were healthy, but all had lost weight. They talked about what might happen at the transit camp.

Paul shared what he'd heard from one of the prisoners on an outside detail. "They're letting anyone who's not a threat leave, like the old men in the Volkssturm and teenagers from the Hitler Youth. The Americans want to be rid of as many of us as they can. They have more prisoners than expected, not anticipating how many of us would surrender to them to avoid the Russians."

"From what I've heard they'll release people with certain skills first," said Rudi, "like farmers and people who can build and fix things. You, Heinz, should tell them that you worked on your uncle's farm or that you speak good English. If we learned one thing from here, it's that the Amis could use more translators."

They continued to talk over ideas and possible stories they could tell when they were officially processed, until it was time to sleep.

* * * *

April 21

The order to move came before first light. Gathering their rucksacks and helping Heinz with his, the group moved toward the gate. Wehrmacht officers organized them into four columns and soon hundreds of prisoners streamed out of the camp in long columns, walking west until they reached a road where they found rows of parked army trucks; the ubiquitous deuce and a half. Here American MPs, military police, assumed the job of getting them loaded.

Walking down the columns, one of the MPs counted the rows and then stuck his arm between them, dividing the columns into sections. In broken German he told the first section to take a step forward and ordered them to climb into one of the trucks. Seeing that the dividing line put Bernd and Helmut into a separate section, Rudi watched the MP as he moved down the line. When the MP wasn't looking, Rudi waved his hand for them to step into his group. Two extra wouldn't make any difference. The MP had counted well; they were tightly packed standing up in the back of the open truck.

It was lucky they'd made it on the same truck. As the convoy reached a crossroads, MPs directing traffic at the first intersection sent the trucks behind them to the west, while theirs continued south. Apparently, they were being taken to different camps.

After an hour of driving they reached the transit camp near a town on the Fulda River. It had been a

POW camp for allied airmen during the war. Here Wehrmacht officers and NCOs would manage prisoner work details, but the camp was guarded by the Americans who would shortly begin processing the prisoners; among their objectives would be to find those who served in the SS and war criminals. Before entering the camp they were searched again and then directed to specific barracks.

Walking into their assigned barracks, Helmut let out a sigh of relief, "We're no longer in the open, thank god, and there are washbasins!"

The searches, assigning barracks, and providing a simple meal to the prisoners had taken all day and extended into the night. Rudi and the others were finally able to settle in, minus Heinz. As prisoners entered the camp, men with visible wounds or illnesses were removed from the column and taken to the dispensary. Rudi had informed one of the Wehrmacht officers that Heinz should be examined as he was still in a weakened state.

****

APRIL 29

After a week, life in the camp had settled into a routine. Each barracks was led by a group of Wehrmacht NCOs who assigned work details during morning formation. Prisoners were put to work cooking meals in the kitchen, cleaning the washrooms, and keeping the grounds clean. Some details went outside the camp to clear rubble or help farmers. Gradually the process of being registered and questioning began.

Whenever he could, Rudi asked other soldiers how the process had gone and what questions the Americans asked. One told him, "The usual; my unit, where I had been, what my job was, that sort of thing. They're keen on finding members of the SS and party members; I had to take off my shirt so they could check if I had tattoos."

"Anything else?" asked Rudi.

"They asked about my education, if I had training in carpentry, that sort of thing, and where I lived before the war," he'd answered.

After talking to several more prisoners, Rudi gradually saw the pattern. The Allies were thinking ahead, knowing they would need a work force to manage and rebuild the country. He guessed that anyone with a clear background and the needed skills might be released early, especially if they lived near the camp. He began to formulate a plan for an early release.

The others had settled into various jobs. Heinz, after recovering from his illness, was working as an interpreter, Bernd had easily found work in the motor pool as a mechanic and Helmut was a clerk again. Only Paul and Rudi were at loose ends, leading various details inside the camp.

* * * *

May 1

That morning the news spread through the camp that the Russians had surrounded Berlin and that Hitler was dead. It caused a stir, but more so among the hardcore believers scattered among the prisoners. They had been a problem back at the first camp, often causing fights and accusing other prisoners of being traitors for believing that the war was lost. When they could, the Americans had separated them from the other prisoners, placing them together. Most of the prisoners knew it was over, but still many found it hard to comprehend after almost six years of sacrifice.

* * * *

May 9

At morning formation, it was announced that the day before, May 8th, Germany had surrendered. For most, the news was received as inevitable and quickly sprung a new crop of rumors, although it was still unclear what would happen to them. Many hoped that they would be released soon as a result.

Later in the day, Rudi and the others sat together in the mess hall, pondering the fact that they were alive—they'd survived the war! To date, none of them had been questioned, and given the hundreds of prisoners yet to process, it might take weeks if not months before they had their turn. For the moment, the thought of going back to their former lives and families seemed alien.

Rudi shared his view, "I think they will release those who either live close to the camp first, or have skills needed to build up the country again. Everything outside of this camp is broken. Nothing is really working. There're thousands of refugees wandering around trying to get home. I heard about one of the forced labor camps being liberated and the workers just walked out, wandering about searching for food. Its chaos and the Americans don't want us adding to it."

Paul nodded his agreement. "Look, here's what we're thinking. As officers, Rudi and I have volunteered to lead work details outside of the camp. It's clear that for now being a weather technician is low on the list of needed jobs. It's all about carpenters, plumbers and the like, mechanics like you, Bernd, and translators like Heinz. People like Helmut are needed to keep things on track. So, Rudi and I needed to come up with a plan. By leading details outside, we can find out about the towns around the camp and life there in general. So that when our interviews come, the Americans can be convinced that we're from one of the nearby towns. It's a way for us to get out sooner."

Rudi added, "There's been some rumors that prisoners will be sent to France or England to help rebuild there. To me that means being a POW for much longer, maybe a long time. We don't know. Getting out sooner is our best bet."

The others listened in silence. They'd worked together at the airfield for over a year and had then undertaken a dangerous journey together to get them here. They had forged a strong bond and the idea of now going their separate ways was new—inevitable, but hard to contemplate at the moment.

Helmut broke the silence, "Rudi, of all the people I've ever met, you are a life artist; you know how to survive and what to do in any situation. You are probably right, everything has an end; only a sausage has two."

Paul chuckled at that, "Who said that, Marcus Aurelius?"

"No, my father!" Helmut said, as they all laughed, but there was now a different sense of what lay ahead for them as they walked out of the mess hall.

* * * *

July 1

Well before war's end the Allies had made plans to divide Germany into four occupation zones managed by an Allied Control Council made up of Britain, France, the Soviet Union and the United States. Now that hostilities had ceased, the occupation was evolving and each zone began to grapple with administrating their respective areas and confronting the myriad problems that arise from governing a war-torn country.

The Allies had taken control of all German media and created new radio stations and newspapers. From the radio, Rudi heard about plans to move the Polish border westward, with parts of Germany east of the Oder River reverting to Poland and the Soviets absorbing the eastern part, effectively shifting the whole country westward.

From what he could gather, this meant that his village would end up in the Soviet occupation zone and inside Poland when the new borders became finalized. He had not heard from his parents, sisters or his wife and daughter. He was anxious to get out of the camp, but so far his interrogation was still pending, as was Paul's. Over the past weeks they'd each led work details outside the camp, taking the opportunity to question local residents, and had shared what they heard with each other. They hoped that now they had enough information to claim that they had lived nearby before the war.

* * * *

July 15

After morning formation, the list of the day's interrogations was posted and this time Rudi's name was on it. He was to report at the specified time to the camp's headquarters, which housed the American occupation forces staff, and to bring his documents.

A lieutenant and a sergeant conducted the interrogation. Sitting at the table across from Rudi, they closely examined his military ID and flight logs, and compared them with his answers to their questions: the extent of his military service, whether he was a Nazi party member or not and what his views were now. From their questions it was clear that they were looking for members of the SS, ranking party members and war criminals.

They asked only a few questions about his so-called "hometown". What played in his favor was that he'd been at sea for much of the years when the Nazis came to power and that his primary role in the war had been as weather technician in the Luftwaffe. But the sergeant was somewhat skeptical of Rudi's claim he'd lived in Kassel.

"Your merchant marine papers indicate you consistently shipped out of ports in northern Germany," he pointed out. Rudi explained he'd always wanted to go to sea and that during the Depression there had been no opportunities for work in Kassel. Going to sea was the only option at the time. The lieutenant and the sergeant remained skeptical and looked at him silently for awhile, until the lieutenant finally shrugged and dismissed Rudi. He was to watch the list posted outside the office of those to be discharged.

Leaving the building, Rudi could feel the sweat in the small of his back from the lengthy interrogation, but he felt that his ruse might work. Once he had his discharge papers in hand, the next challenge would be to make it all the way to Hamburg, crossing a war-torn country whose railroads and other transportation were, if not destroyed, severely disrupted. He'd have to find food and shelter along the way; and might have to pass through towns where the general civil order had broken down.

* * * *

July 30

Every morning Rudi checked the roster, standing in the crowd as everyone searched the list for their names. Amongst the murmurs of disappointment was the occasional quiet cheer that someone had found his name on the roster. He noticed that, over time, the number of released prisoners was actually increasing, giving credence to the rumor that the Allies wanted as many of them as possible to return to the workforce and help rebuild the country.

As he was finishing his lunch in the mess hall, Rudi saw Helmut approaching looking very excited. "Rudi, your name is on the list and so is Paul's!" he exclaimed. "They just now posted a second list!"

For a moment Rudi wasn't sure he'd heard correctly, "What? Are you sure?"

"Yes, I am," insisted Helmut. "And now that we're seeing the releases picking up, maybe all of us will be out of here soon!"

"What happens next?" Rudi asked.

"Go to the building next to headquarters. They're only open in the afternoon. You present yourself, sign the roster that you've received your papers, and if you're lucky they'll give you some civilian clothing. If you need more, use some of your cigarettes to buy some."

People are creatures of habit. The group had adapted to the camp's routine and they were relatively comfortable. Each had a job to do and was paid a small amount for doing it and, while not plentiful by any measure, there was food. Suddenly, now about to be released, everything would change for Rudi and Paul. They would face a new challenge, one they'd been thinking about for months.

That night the group celebrated. On their outside work details, Rudi and Paul had traded their cigarettes for clothes; a shirt here, a pair of pants there, and now each had a complete outfit. They'd also managed a small bottle of schnapps, which they passed around sans glasses.

Rudi knew that Paul had his doubts about making the journey to Hamburg once they were released, feeling it was dangerous and uncertain what would await him there. He also hadn't been confident that he could convince the American interrogators that he was from Kassel. So before his interrogation, while they were on outside details, Paul had investigated finding work in Kassel; if something came up he could stay until the situation in the country improved. His university studies as a meteorologist had included classes in chemistry, and he knew of a temporary position in the town's public works department. His working knowledge of English and his science education would make him a good intermediary between the German staff and the Americans overseeing the administration. He had brought up the idea in his interrogation and it had seemed well received, although he didn't know until today that it had been approved.

Across the occupation zone, the Americans wanted town administrators to remain in their jobs to provide services to their populations. They needed trained people to ensure that facilities such as the municipal water supply functioned and were safe, as well as provided public health services to prevent epidemics. The shortage of personnel trained to handle these jobs and the need to work with the American occupation officials made Paul a good fit.

Heinz leaned over to Rudi. "If you make it to the car on your way back, I hid the revolver under the front seat. If you showed up at my uncle's farm they could use your help and give you a place to stay for awhile. That Herbert is probably gone and sitting in a camp somewhere."

Rudi nodded, "Good idea, Heinz. I'll have to see how it goes."

* * * *

August 2

At noon, Helmut, Bernd, Heinz and Paul stood by the gate to see Rudi off. Other than to promise to stay in touch and wish him luck, nobody said anything. They shook hands silently as they had done back at the airfield and watched as Rudi pulled on his rucksack and strode out of the camp.

* * * *

August 3

When Rudi left the camp he carried a small food package given to everyone discharged and a canteen of water. He spent his first night of freedom in a field outside Rothenburg. Waking before sunrise, he walked into the town as he considered his options. His plan was to head straight north toward Hamburg. He still had his apartment in Stade and knew the town hadn't been bombed, except for the airfield on the outskirts where he had taken his military training. Getting there was the question, which was answered the moment he saw a bicycle leaning next to a house with several others. It was still very early and no one was around. Without thinking about it, in one quick motion he pushed the bicycle into the street, swung his leg over the seat and began pedaling, not bothering to see if anyone was chasing him.

He'd originally planned to walk into town, cross to the east side of the Fulda river and then northward to see if the car was still there. Instead, after taking the bicycle, he changed his mind—he would stay on the west side and made his way up to Kassel. He could cross there.

Throughout the day he passed groups of refugees walking along the roadside carrying what they could save from their former home; a bollerwagen with children sitting atop packed belongings, wagons pulled by horses, even cows. Some had fled the Russian advance during the war; others were leaving the nearby Soviet sector. It was the same as their drive from the airfield; the war and its aftermath had created chaos and scattered people in every direction.

Nearing a town south of Kassel, he could see from a distance that the streets were full of people milling about. Wondering what was going on he stopped next to a house where a woman was hanging out her family's laundry to dry and greeted her.

"Why are so many people there?" asked Rudi.

Without looking at him, she replied, "They are DPs, displaced people, workers from one of the labor camps. Most are Poles. They came here for jobs during the war; others came later, those that were forced to work."

"Do they make trouble?" Rudi asked.

The woman looked at him for the first time and said, "They don't bother me, but some can be trouble, especially if they think you are a guard from one of the camps or SS. Then you better watch out." She squinted at him as if to guess if he was or not. "Otherwise they wander around trying to find food and wanting to go home, like everyone else. The Americans bring in food, but it's not enough."

Rudi thanked her and got back on the bicycle. He could circumvent the town, but decided to bluff his way through. There had been Poles near his village working the harvest season on the big farms and Rudi knew a few words of Polish. He hoped they wouldn't take him for a former SS soldier; once again the SS presented him with problems. Taking a deep breath, he rolled into the town.

Nearing the first group of men he tipped his hat and said, "Dzien dobry" (good day). The men turned briefly to look at Rudi, returned his greeting, and then resumed their conversation. He continued riding through the town, giving a wave or wishing someone good day until he was on the other side.

There was no reason to go into Kassel. During the war it had been bombed and the final battle for the city had brought further destruction. Like many other cities, it would be packed with refugees seeking shelter and food. Northeast of the town the Americans had erected an amphibious bridge that he could use to cross the Weser. Rudi still entertained the thought of trying to find the car, locate some gas for it and drive northward. He felt he could manage the driving, having watched Heinz. But the moment he crossed the bridge he'd be in the British zone with a checkpoint, as traffic between the occupation zones was controlled. His discharge papers limited him to the American zone, and so he decided to head north to Hofgeismar, just short of the British occupation border. There it might be easier to find an uncontrolled place to cross.

Alongside the road he could see people working in the fields. His small packet of food was gone and he was hungry. My best bet is to work for something to eat on a farm, he thought. But with so many people wandering about, the first farmer he approached seemed suspicious of him, "We have enough workers and little food. The next farm up the road might need help. The family's sons are still POWs."

He thanked the farmer and rode up the road to the next one. There the farmer was cautious, "Yes, we need help, but we don't need people who'll eat our food and then not know what to do or work hard. Tell me what you know about farming. Can you handle a team of horses?"

Satisfied with Rudi's answers, the farmer told him to settle in the bunk room for field hands, although currently there were none, and to get some food from the main kitchen. "My name is Wilhelm and my wife is Helga. After you eat something, find me and I'll show you what I need done."

* * * *

SEPTEMBER 1

With the steady diet and physical work Rudi had begun to gain weight again. Wilhelm appreciated Rudi's hard work and skill at farming, and they got along well.

"Watching you I can see you grew up on farm," Wilhelm had remarked. They had spent the month cutting hay, every day, all day long, steadily swinging scythes, one behind the other, but overlapping, moving up and down the field in rows. Then they led horses pulling large drag rakes to fluff the hay so it could dry. Once dry, it was gathered into bundles to take to the barn. It was hot and dusty work, interrupted only when Helga came out with lunch and cool water.

In the evenings Helga would join them for schnapps, and Rudi would tell stories of his years at sea. In turn, Wilhelm filled Rudi in on what was happening in the occupation zones.

"We know some farmers over there—in the Soviet sector; they are doing things differently than the Americans," Wilhelm explained. "The Russian is taking everything, you know, dismantling factories and anything that can be moved and shipping it back to Russia. Of course, we destroyed a lot there too, but they're also confiscating our farms. That Stalin wants to take over all of Germany, I think. It'll be hard for the people over there. It's not clear what the Allies will do, but here at least the Americans and the British are trying to get things going again."

"It's out of our control, Wilhelm," Helga said. "I just want our boys back, hopefully soon! We received a letter from the Red Cross. They are both in America, you know, some place called New Mexico saying that the Amis actually let them study there. Our eldest has even been taking classes to be an engineer!"

Wilhelm chuckled, "I wasn't surprised when I read that. Our Peter didn't like farming; did his chores alright, but never took to it, since he preferred books. Not like Alfred, he was born for it, like me."

"Mm, that's very true," smiled Helga.

Wilhelm turned to Rudi, "I know you want to get back to Hamburg or wherever it is, but you are welcome to stay here. You've been a big help to us."

"Thanks Wilhelm, but I need to find my family and get settled. I've appreciated being able to stay here and your generosity."

Wilhelm nodded, "Ah, of course we understand. When you're ready to leave I'll go with you and show you where to cross into the British sector. A good friend has a farm whose fields are on both sides. It's not far."

* * * *

September 7

It was still dark as Rudi packed his few belongings into the rucksack, including a food package Helga had put together for him. Wilhelm pushed his bicycle out of the barn and stood as Rudi said goodbye to Helga, thanking her. "I hope your sons are back soon."

"Thank you, Rudi, I wish you much luck and visit us if you are ever near here," Helga said quietly.

Together Rudi and Wilhelm rode north, passing people walking along the road. Occasionally, a truck filled with American soldiers overtook them, stirring up dust. Arriving at his friend's farm, Wilhelm introduced Rudi to Johan and explained what Rudi wanted to do.

Johan shrugged, "Fine with me. Take him to the lower cow pasture. The British sector runs between the two slopes. I'd go with you, but I'm caught up with a cow delivering a calf. Wilhelm knows where it is."

Rudi thanked him and followed Wilhelm to the barn where he parked his bicycle. "You'll have to walk your bicycle from here," he told Rudi. They headed into the field and walked until they came to the crest of a long, steep slope. Wilhelm pointed, "That slope over there, is where you want to go. Keep off the main road for a few kilometers once you are across; the English patrol behind their checkpoint. There are paths everywhere; just keep north and you'll be fine."

"Thanks, I have a map and compass, so that'll help," said Rudi.

"No way to get lost then," chuckled Wilhelm as he reached into his pocket and handed Rudi some folded Reichsmarks. "Here, this might be useful. They've fixed sections of the railroad and have some trains running again. Maybe in Hannover, I'm not sure."

Rudi wanted to refuse the money, but all he had was what he'd earned in the transit camp and it wasn't much. He thanked Wilhelm for the money. They shook hands and Rudi walked his bicycle down the long slope and up the other side. At the crest he turned around and in the far distance he could see Wilhelm with his arm up and slowly waving. Rudi waved back, then turned and walked down the far side of the slope.

* * * *

September 15

Finally: Hamburg. Rudi had ridden into the city on a freight train, hoping to find an old friend from his merchant marine days.

The last week had been a challenge. After leaving Wilhelm, he'd considered retracing some of the route the group had driven and head for Heinz's uncle's farm, especially as the weather was now colder and raining on and off. He finally decided to keep on a direct route. Passing through a series of towns, he wished he could have recovered Heinz's revolver. There were refugees, displaced persons and former forced laborers everywhere from any number of countries roaming about. Rudi heard stories of assaults and robberies. He didn't have any trouble and doubted some of the stories he heard, but looking at the bombed out houses with people living among the ruins, it was clear some would be desperate enough to do whatever it took to survive.

It was for the best anyway. As he rode his bicycle through Hannover to the train station, he had to pass through a British checkpoint. Luckily, the soldiers were overwhelmed trying to keep up with the long lines of people wanting to pass. When his turn came, the soldiers focused on searching Rudi's rucksack and only gave his discharge papers a glance, but lectured him on the need to register with British authorities immediately upon his return home. Had they found the revolver, he would surely have been arrested.

In Hannover he learned that the rumor about trains running to Hamburg was true. Since the end of the war, railway engineers had managed to repair key rail lines by relocating track and equipment from damaged lines and those with a low priority. The Allies, with German labor, were working to get the railways functioning so that they could transport much-needed food and supplies to the population.

The limited service meant overcrowding. The station was packed with people and their baggage. Rudi slowly made his way through the throng to the ticket counter. He asked which train was heading for Hamburg. The man behind the counter turned and pointed to a row of rail cars on the far side of the rail yard. "That one, it's on a side track. It leaves in the morning if the tracks are clear and comes into platform five."

"Is there room for a bicycle?" asked Rudi.

"Most of the train is made of freight cars, toward the rear, so there's room for a bicycle. You have to be fast. When the passenger cars fill up, people pack into the freight cars; some even sit on top."

Rudi wanted to keep the bicycle, but it would be a hindrance getting on the train in the middle of a rushing crowd. Just moving through the train station was difficult enough with people sitting here and there, their bundles strewn about. He had to spend the night nearby or in the station until the morning. Outside the station late at night seemed risky. He could get robbed or have his bicycle stolen.

The best thing to do was get to the train first, he thought. Lifting the bicycle on this shoulder, he walked out of the station toward the train. As he crossed over rows of railroad tracks, he passed small groups of children carrying sacks and filled with chunks of coal that had fallen off freight cars to take back to their homes or sell. Some looked barely ten years old. They ignored him as he walked alongside the row of rail cars until he found an open freight car. Lifting the bicycle inside, he climbed in after it and settled in for the night.

* * * *

Rudi was awakened by a loud bang and the jerk of the freight car, followed by a rapid series of smaller bangs. A locomotive had hooked up and was pressing the hitches on the freight cars together. With the slack out of the hitches, the locomotive now began to slowly pull the freight cars one at a time, then the next, each car moving in succession. The train rolled away from the station for several minutes until it reached the junction that led back to the station. The process repeated itself as it stopped with a lurch, the cars banging together. Reversing direction the train rolled toward the station, the wheels screeched and squealed as they crossed over adjacent tracks, making the train rock. Looking out the open door of the freight car, Rudi saw that the platform was packed with people and their baggage ready to board. It would have been impossible to get on with his bicycle.

* * * *

Rudi wasn't sure he could find Siggi, assuming he was still alive. Hamburg had been devastated from the firebombing, and piles of rubble lined the roads into the city and along the streets. He wandered the crowded streets as people went about their business and children played amongst the rubble; hoping to find something of value that could be sold or traded. Thousands had been displaced, and the likelihood he'd find anyone he knew was slim, but he wanted to try before heading home to Stade.

The area where Siggi lived was unrecognizable, as most landmarks were gone. Rudi wasn't even sure if he had the right street. Walking his bicycle, he began reading the notes written in chalk on the walls and signs tacked on the damaged buildings; informing anyone looking for the previous residents where they could be found. He stopped an old woman walking along the street and asked her if she knew of someone named Siggi, a merchant marine sailor. At first she said no, she didn't know anyone by that name. Rudi then described what he looked like and mentioned that his real name was Siegfried. Thinking on it, the woman recalled a man with that name who lived on the block, farther down the street in an apartment. She didn't know if he was alive, though.

Rudi thanked her and continued down the street, scanning the notices and chalked messages. Eventually, he found a note signed with the name 'Siegfried', stating that the person had relocated and an address. If it's him, at least he survived, Rudi said to himself.

He spent some time looking for the address on the note and finally found it, a basement of a damaged building.

Rudi knocked on the door and waited. He recognized Siggi as soon as he opened the door, but it took awhile before Siggi recognized him. "Rudi, my god, you are alive!" he exclaimed, clapping him on the back, "Come in, it's not much, but it's comfortable."

Siggi had turned the basement into living quarters with salvaged chairs and a table. There was a small coal stove and two beds.

"This is my parent's house. They're with my sister out in the country," Siggi said. "Much better for them since there's nothing left of it. Here, have a seat, and tell me how you are?"

They talked for awhile about mutual friends they'd been with at sea; if they'd heard any news. But it wasn't time to go over everything; everyone had experienced the war, so what more was there to talk about? The mood now was forward-looking.

They had served on two ships together, and while Rudi thought of Siggi as a scoundrel in his own right; he was never sure if Siggi was connected to the criminal underworld or just a good smuggler. But he knew he was a good sailor and could be trusted. In the 1930s, during the Spanish Civil War, it was Siggi who had found him a spot on a freighter that was smuggling weapons from Germany into Franco's Spain. They'd been paid well for that journey.

Recalling the trip, Rudi told Siggi, "When I first boarded that ship, I thought, what I have gotten myself into? The ship was so rusty you could have thrown a wrench through the hull!"

Siggi laughed, "I remember, but it paid well, didn't it? You thought most of the crew were crooks! Well, some actually were; but you know as well as I do that you find all kinds of characters on a ship. You always went your own way though. We respected that."

Rudi then proceeded to tell Siggi what he had in mind. "I need your help. Look, everything runs on the black market now, even though the police and Allies try to stop it. It was that way in the POW camp, and it's the same out here. You can't buy enough with ration books. Cigarettes are money, as you know. The Allies aren't going to favor us, that is for sure and dump a lot of food on us. Right now there's not enough anyway. They haven't even decided what to do with Germany yet. We are left to our own devices."

"That's true," nodded Siggi.

"So we have to find ways through by ourselves," said Rudi. "I'm not sure what work there is for me back home, so I want to find things to sell or trade. Do you still have your old contacts?"

"Yes, I know of a couple who survived," replied Siggi. "In fact, one is over in Bremerhaven; it's part of the American sector. Did you know they took over the port there even though this is the British zone?"

"I didn't know," Rudi answered. "Alright then, when I get home I'll let you know how things are."

Siggi nodded, "We'll see soon enough then. Meanwhile, stay the night here, it's starting to rain. Better weather tomorrow. And welcome back!"

Before Rudi left the next day, Siggi handed him two slim beige colored cardboard packets. Holding them in his hand, Rudi read the words Lucky Strike on the side of each one. "Ah, these are American cigarettes. Wonderful!"

"Yes!" exclaimed Siggi. "Those came from American C-rations. Inside there're a couple of small cans; you know, meat, crackers, that sort of thing, plus the four cigarettes—even gum and little packets of coffee. I can get more, so take those, you can use them. It's what most people want."

Siggi was willing to help Rudi do business on the blackmarket, but he also warned him, "If you are going to smuggle you'll have to watch yourself. It's a bit lawless right now and you have to watch out. Plus, the police are always trying to arrest anyone for smuggling."

* * * *

JULY 1946

When Rudi finally arrived home from Hamburg, he found a couple living in his apartment. The local housing authority had assigned it to them. Those who had been bombed out, like the couple, received priority for housing when there was space available. Rudi's apartment had been empty since he'd sent his wife and daughter to live in the east during the war; now they were in the Soviet sector. He moved in with the couple, and they all made the best of it.

Rudi was able to find work in the town's fish market part of the week and sometimes went out to help fish. The market was in a square next to the old town, which was connected to the Elbe by a small tributary. The town had escaped being bombed, leaving the old houses in the center of town intact.

Gutting and cleaning fish brought back memories of his family's fishery, and while familiar, he had to laugh—I left my village because I didn't want to do this anymore! He shrugged, things would get better. Letters came in the mail and he was relieved to find out that his parents and sisters were all right. But his brother-in-law, Willy, married to Frieda, had been captured by the Russians in the last months of the war.

Looking for more work, he managed to obtain a certificate and license "under the table" to work as a salesperson. War or no war, official rules still applied, but the times also made it necessary to find ways around the onerous ones. And so he became a door-to-door salesman, selling pots and pans on his off days from the fish market.

With every sort of basic necessity in short supply, repurposing became the order of the day. What at one time had military application was reconfigured for civilian use. Machine shops trimmed helmets and stamped them into the shape of pots and colanders. Tailors altered a military jacket to give it a civilian style. Until manufacturing could start up, people invented what they needed.

Working at the fish market and selling door to door put him contact in with many people, offering him other chances to make money. In addition to things they needed, people also had wants—among them were cigarettes and alcohol. Once a week, Rudi took the hour-long train ride into Hamburg to buy cigarettes from Siggi. Sometimes his friend only had the small packets from C-rations, other times full packs of Lucky Strikes and Chesterfields, and sometimes bottles of alcohol. Both were highly sought after and easy to sell at the fish market or when he was selling pots and pans door to door. Of course, Siggi made a profit selling them to Rudi, but he gave Rudi a good price so he could also make a profit when he resold them.

He didn't know what arrangement Siggi had with the American GIs in Bremerhaven and didn't want to know. But he suspected that among other things, it included weapons, especially Lugers or anything with a swastika on it as the GIs coveted them for memorabilia. Rudi often wondered if his Luger had ended up in some GI's duffel bag and was now somewhere in America.

It had been a year of adapting. Travel between the occupation zones was restricted, although that didn't stop people crossing over at uncontrolled parts of the borders. Rudi had written to his wife that he could get her and his daughter out of the Soviet zone. Despite being estranged, he wanted to do whatever he could, especially for his daughter. The marriage had effectively ended during the war, needing only to have divorce papers filed. He eventually received a letter from his wife that they would remain in the Soviet zone. That left only the divorce to become official, a process that was going to take time under the post-war circumstances.

* * * *

The occupation zones were changing, and earlier policies by the Allies were being revised. The Soviet sector was placing greater restrictions along their border, while the British and Americans were making plans to reduce restrictions and merge their zones. To travel between the zones a special permit was needed, especially to cross to or from the Soviet zone.

One day, a woman came to the fish market and Rudi recognized her shopping bag, woven out of newspapers like Anna's. A week earlier, he'd received a letter from Else, his younger sister. She was in the Soviet zone and wanted to get to the West. Could Rudi help her? He'd written back that he knew someone who might help.

* * * *

The end of July had been very hot and Anna was glad to be home. She was very tired from being up all night, having just returned from crossing the border between the Soviet and British zones. She gone across in the evening and only made it home very early in the morning. To help the family's business, she'd turned to smuggling on the black market like so many others. Her hometown was only a few kilometers from the border, making it an ideal location for smuggling. Items available on one side could be sold at a higher price or traded for something better in another. When ration cards ran out, everyone turned to the black market for what they needed or wanted.

An old school friend of Anna's worked in the town's administration office that issued ration cards, and she often gave Anna an extra ration card under the table to purchase liquor. With the extra card, Anna would buy all the liquor she could carry in a suitcase and slip across the border to sell it, sharing some of the profit with her school friend. Occasionally, she'd stay with relatives who lived in the British zone before returning in the early morning darkness. Marianne, Anna's sister, used a fairly secure crossing through a dense forest outside of town; however, you had to know exactly where to go as there were swamps and people had drowned there.

Anna's home was near a village that was even closer to the border. She'd go there in the evening and sit in the only café and wait for nightfall. As the evening progressed, the café would fill with people planning to cross for business or to leave the Soviet zone permanently. The trick was to not be caught by the Russian soldiers that patrolled it; as crossing anywhere other than at border control points with an inter-zone permit was illegal. Keeping up with changes at the border was important. These were whispered around, including where best to cross and how the patrols were timed. The border was patrolled by Russian draftees from somewhere in Russia's hinterland; many almost illiterate.

Anna was caught once crossing over. Thinking quickly, she resisted as best she could, and although she was beaten and had her bottles taken, she escaped sexual assault by telling the soldiers she had syphilis. She continued to cross the border, but alternated locations, often choosing her sister's favorite spot.

Anna could always tell when she was back in the Soviet zone—by the smell. The Allied sectors used black coal which was of better quality, while in the East brown coal was used. It was of lower quality and gave off a slightly sweet smell.

Walking up stairs to the family's rooms above their shop, she was greeted by her mother. "Hello my dear, I'm so glad you are back safe. I always worry. By the way, you have mail; it came yesterday while you were over there," making a motion with her head as she handed the envelope to her.

Turning the letter over, Anna was surprised to see from the return address that it was from Rudi. She told her mother, "I'll read it later. But first, I have a surprise!" Pulling out the Reichsmarks from selling the liquor she placed them on the table. Then she opened her suitcase to pull out a large ham hock and excitedly told her mother, "I traded for this! It should last us awhile, you think?"

Her mother reached for the ham hock and smelled it, "Oh my, this is wonderful! Thank you for bringing it. By the way, your father wanted you to find him when you got back."

"Where is he? I didn't see him in the shop when I came in," she asked.

They heard a sharp pop and then another. Her mother briefly rolled her eyes, "That's him, down under the house shooting rats with his pistol. He found some near the cellar with the potatoes; there must be a hole in the brickwork somewhere. He could just fix it, instead of always going down there to shoot them. It doesn't help."

"I think," mused Anna, "he likes it that way. I'll find him when he is done."

"Maybe you are right, but still," her mother remarked.

Anna left for her room in the attic. She'd shared it with Marianne growing up until her sister had married. The attic wasn't insulated, and so in winter the two of them slept under thick goose down comforters to ward off the cold, sometimes finding a thin layer of ice in their chamber pots.

She sat in her favorite chair and opened Rudi's letter. After updating her on his current situation, she came to the part asking for her to help to bring his sister across the border. He'd included an address were Else could be reached, thinking it best if Anna wrote her directly to save time.

The next day Anna wrote Rudi to tell him she'd written Else and would take her across the border; she could come along on one of her black market runs. In her letter to Else she mentioned that coming sooner would be better; there were rumors that the Russians were making changes at the border that would make it more difficult and dangerous to cross. Else could stay with them until the timing was right.

* * * *

SEPTEMBER 1946

Else came in early September. Anna had heard enough stories from Rudi about what it was like working on their family farm and fishing, including stories about his favorite sister that she felt that she already knew Else. She was used to hard work and would be fine making the crossing. It took a few days for Anna to collect enough liquor to make the trip worthwhile. The weather was good and with a partial moon that night it was the ideal time to go.

Shortly before leaving, Anna told Else what had happened when she was caught crossing. "You already know how things are for women, but I wanted to warn you. There's another place, it's my sister's favorite, but it's swampy and people have drowned there. I think it's best to use my spot; I could walk it with my eyes closed. The sentry schedule I have is up to date so we should be fine."

Else said she understood and related her experience fleeing in front of the Russian advance during the war. "I was on one of the last trains trying to get west. Fighter planes would strafe the train, so that when they started to dive down the train would slam on the brakes so everyone could jump off and run into the fields. It happened twice, so I feel lucky!" They left that night and crossed without incident.

* * * *

At home, Anna settled into the routine of working in her parent's store. She watched her nephew whenever her sister was away from home. They had a small contract to make caps for the Russian garrison in town, and were glad they could keep their two workers busy sewing the caps. Since coming back, she'd connected with her old girlfriends and they often met at her house. If they stayed past curfew, Anna would walk them home and get herself back. She knew what back alleys to take and was less afraid of being caught than were her girlfriends.

All and all, a sense of some normalcy was returning. Until one day, two Russian soldiers came into the store, obviously drunk. One had a torn cap and needed it repaired. Anna's mother was in the store and after examining the cap, which was filthy, refused to sew it until it was clean. Words ensued until Anna's father came out from the workshop and agreed to sew it. Problem solved, it seemed.

An hour later, a Russian sergeant entered the shop with the two soldiers demanding to see Anna's mother. Having heard what had happened, Anna tried to explain the situation to the sergeant. "Be quiet!" he bellowed and chopped her in the neck with the edge of his hand, laying her out on the floor. They then arrested her mother for having resisted the orders of the Soviet occupation authority by refusing to fix the cap. Her mother was taken to the Russian headquarters and placed in a cell in the basement of the building.

Anna was beside herself, immediately grabbed her coat and walked to the headquarters. There she was able to talk to the commander and explain what happened. To her surprise he was sympathetic; yes, he could see his how his soldiers had overreacted and would look into the matter. Later that evening her mother was released. It had been a telling experience; the Russians would be taking a different approach to occupation than in the western sectors.

* * * *

January 1947

Coming home from shopping, Anna put down her bag, shook the snow off her coat and hung it up to dry in the hallway. Stepping into the workshop she briefly greeted her father, who was stretching a hat to re-size it. In the workshop were several wooden forms the size and shape of a human head that were used to size hats. Made from hardwood, the forms had wooden screws embedded in movable sections. By turning the screws, different sections allowed the head to expand, thus stretching the hat. She could hear voices upstairs and wondered who was her mother talking to? Her father was in the workshop and her sister was at her home. She grabbed her bag and climbed up the narrow steps.

Stepping into the living room, which was warm from the coal stove. She couldn't believe her eyes, there sitting on the couch was Rudi. Her mother was pouring him tea and encouraging him to help himself to cake. That in of itself showed Anna that her mother was charmed by him.

* * * *

APRIL 1947

When he'd visited Anna in January, it was not only a chance for Rudi to thank her for bringing his sister over to the west, but to see her. The end of the war had interrupted their relationship, leaving a question mark for both of them.

After that first visit, Rudi started making regular visits to see her. He'd also found that there was a demand for American cigarettes in the Soviet zone. Leaving the cigarettes at relatives of Anna's family in the west, he'd enter the Soviet zone legally and have his inter-zone permit stamped, allowing a stay of 30 days. Then he'd illegally cross the border to the west with Anna and pick them up to sell in the east zone. In the intervening time they'd cross the border multiple times, smuggling whatever they could until it was time for Rudi to leave the zone legally, repeating the process a few weeks later. On some occasions Siggi was able to provide Rudi with nylon stockings to sell. These were in high demand by women and easy to carry.

That August, Anna and Rudi married and moved to Stade. They hired a farmer whose fields were in the restricted zone to bring across their furniture using his horse and wagon. Anna's father gave them his old motorcycle as a wedding gift, which they pushed over the border. The motorcycle took patience to operate; it had a weak headlight limiting its use at night, especially when it was raining and the engine's two inline cylinders meant the rear cylinder often overheated, forcing them to stop and let it cool. Nonetheless, Rudi made good use of it as he continued working at the fish market and selling his pots and pans door to door.

* * * *

JUNE 1948

That month, dramatic events within days of each other would change Anna and Rudi's fortunes. At the beginning of the month they'd stopped off in Hamburg to visit Siggi on their way home after another trip into the Soviet sector. From Siggi they first heard the rumors that the British and American zones would be officially merged and that a new currency would be introduced.

"Sometime this month the British and Amis will replace the Reichsmark with the new Deutschmark," explained Siggi, "and not at a good exchange I hear."

"What do you mean? What is it?" asked Anna.

"As far as I know, the exchange will be ten Reichsmarks for one new Deutschmark. They say there is too much paper money in the banks. During the war we couldn't buy much and everything was rationed; so we just let it build up. It isn't worth much and no one really wants them— that's what makes the black market work," said Siggi.

"On top of that the Americans printed their own occupation marks," said Rudi. "They're worried we'll have inflation again like in the 1920s and the mess that followed."

"Even though our savings will be reduced, everyone will receive 40 Deutschmarks as a start," added Siggi.

"The Russians will be angry," said Anna. "They already fight with the Allies about what to do with Germany. Now the Allies are going their own way. The Russians will go another."

"Mmm, I'm not a banker, that's for sure," acknowledged Rudi, "but I think this will end the black market and put the three of us out of business."

"Really?" asked Anna.

Siggi nodded, "I agree with Rudi. Once it happens and there is a real currency that people have confidence in, it'll wipe out the Reichsmark making it worthless. Then the days of buying things with cigarettes is probably done as well, I'm pretty sure of that. I know from my contacts that shops have held back all sorts of hard-to-get goods. As soon as there is a new currency I bet the shelves fill up. Why sell them for worthless currency when you can finally get real money?"

Later that month the changes were announced. The speed with which it was instituted showed that it had been thoroughly planned and in secret—the new Deutschmarks having been printed in the United States. The Western powers would unify their occupation zones, create a new German state and commit to rebuilding the country.

* * * *

Coming home from selling his pots and pans, Rudi told Anna what he'd seen, "I went by the market on the way home and there are all sorts of new goods on the shelves with prices in Deutschmarks. I couldn't believe my eyes! And they're not especially cheap, either."

"So, Siggi was right," said Anna.

A few days later their neighbors, Mr. Schulz and his wife knocked on their door. "Have you heard the news on the radio?" asked Mr. Schulz in an excited voice.

Rudi and Anna shook their heads, "No, what's happened?'

Mr. Schulz related what they'd heard, "The Russians have blockaded Berlin! The railways and roads—even the canals! They don't want anything to get into Berlin. It's crazy! There are over two million people there"

"My god, maybe there will be another war," shuddered Mrs. Schulz.

"Let's hope not," interjected Mr. Schulz, "Right now they are mad about the unification and the new Deutschmark. The Russians think they can force the Allies to back down and give up on Berlin. On the radio they said they will print their own money now."

* * * *

June 1948

Not wanting Berlin to be absorbed by the Russians, the British immediately started an airlift to supply the city, soon followed by the Americans. It would take thousands of tons of supplies to maintain the city.

On his way home from the fish market, Rudi picked up their mail. Walking up to their apartment, he sifted through the letters finding one from his older sister Frieda, another from Anna's mother and the last one from the British occupation authorities.

"Anna, you have a letter," he said. "And there's this one." He held it up for her to see.

"What do you think it's about?" she wondered.

Rudi shrugged as he opened the envelope, reading it in silence as Anna waited impatiently and finally asked, "Well?"

Rudi looked up with a big smile and hugged her, "It's good news! Here read it."

As Anna scanned the letter she became more and more excited, "Amazing! They want you back, all of you."

The letter included a directive from the German government calling back to duty many of the meteorologists and weather technicians that had served in the German Weather Service during the war. At the bottom was a request to report for an orientation in Hamburg in seven days.

The airlift had quickly become a monumental task and needed all kinds of skills to make it work; paramount was having the resources to forecast the weather to ensure safe operations.

Anna smiled at Rudi and said, "I'd say your time as a salesman and working at the fish market is over, you think?"

Rudi nodded, "Yes, maybe so and good timing, our black market days are done for sure. Siggi was right; currency reform will stabilize things and bring an end to our little business."

* * * *

A week later Rudi found himself sitting in a conference room at Hamburg's airport. The room slowly filled to capacity as former weather personnel who had served all over Europe filed in. A British major called for everyone's attention and introduced the day's agenda. A large map of Germany was pulled down from the ceiling behind him.

The major turned to it, tapped it with his pointer and gave the room his assessment of the situation. "Out of necessity, we've had to quickly expand the airlift, but it's becoming more organized every day. There are hundreds of planes in the air at the same time, and your ability to forecast the weather will be critical to safe operations, especially once winter begins. And yes, we anticipate this will be an extended operation with no end date at this time."

Tapping the map again, the major continued, "Here and here, planes leave from multiple airfields in the West. For safety and efficiency, inbound flights to Tempelhof and Gatow airfields use these two 20-mile-wide corridors, one north and one south—with outbound flights taking the middle corridor."

Not long after the orientation, Rudi soon began working at British Royal Air Force fields as a weather technician, dividing his time between two airports outside of Hamburg. Commuting by train from Stade daily would be difficult, so he stayed during the week at barracks near the airport, returning home on his days off.

Anna and Rudi quickly decided it would be best to move into Hamburg. However, it wasn't as simple as packing up and finding a place. There was a critical shortage of housing from the extensive bombing. The solution was to trade residences, a Ringtausch or exchange.

Coming home one day, Rudi told Anna, "I went to the housing authorities in town and put us on the list for an apartment in Hamburg. Hopefully, there will be a match with someone who wants to move here."

"I'm optimistic," said Anna. "Things have gotten better for us since you started working for the British."

"Yes, that's true," said Rudi. "And soon I'll be going to night school. I'm taking an English translator class in the evening after my shift. It will really help with my work, as only a few of the British speak any German at all."

* * * *

While waiting for a chance to trade their apartment for another in Hamburg, Anna gave birth to their son, Hans. At the same time, Rudi's mother came to live with them.

A year after the war ended, Rudi's mother and father were expelled from their farm and given only hours to pack what little they could take with them and leave. The same was true for most Germans who had ended up in Poland when the border was moved westward.

At first they'd gone to nearby Swinemünde, a city still inside the Soviet zone, to live with relatives. There Rudi's father had died, brought on in part by starvation. With her son and daughters in the west, his mother saw no reason to stay in the Soviet zone. Old friends made arrangements with local fishing folk who smuggled her out by hiding her in the chain locker of a freighter bound for Hamburg in the west.

Finally an apartment became available to trade, the top part of a house in the suburbs of Hamburg. Rudi's mother moved in with Else who had married. Finally released from a Russian POW camp, Rudi's brother-in-law, Willy, rejoined his wife Frieda in the west. He had lost a lot of weight in captivity, and it took Frieda and Rudi's mother a long time to nurse him back to health.

The airlift would last for almost a year and successfully broke the blockade. Airlifts continued for a few months more in case the blockade resumed. It was a remarkable achievement, and Rudi was proud of his role in it. In 1952, Rudi was hired directly to work in the German Weather Service.

But his wartime hope that he could achieve the status of an official meteorologist with his experience was never realized. Now in his early 40s and without a university degree, he would always remain a weather technician. His ambition was greater than that, and it motivated him to seek a different direction. Jochen, a pilot in his squadron that he'd served with in the Arctic was living in Montreal, Canada; and wrote Rudi there's gold in the streets here letters.

In 1953, Rudi, Anna and their son immigrated to Canada. There Rudi studied to become an electrical engineer. With his degree and weather experience he would finally reach his goal of becoming a meteorologist. Rudi never saw his daughter from his first marriage again. Through letters they often heard from the other four escapees.

Heinz had managed to immigrate to America and was in California pursuing his dream of working in the movies. Paul finished his remaining studies and became a meteorologist at Tempelhof airport in Berlin. Paul's nephew Fritz survived the western front and his time as a POW before being released. Bernd returned to his auto repair business, which prospered as the post-war economy improved and more people could afford a car. Bernd's son returned from the POW camp in America, but had to work for a year in England before being officially released. Helmut returned to Heidelberg and became the head administrator for the school system. He and Tutti adopted a boy, a war orphan, and resumed their walks along the Neckar with Plato.

Outside the last town the five had passed through; a farmer returning home after being evacuated found, to his amazement, a Mercedes hidden in the woods next to his fields. He found Bernd's note and inside the car under the front seat a revolver. He dutifully informed the Horst garage in Celle of his find, but kept the revolver.

* * * * * * * * * * *

The author lives in Bellingham, Washington.
This is his first book.